PAUL TEMPLE
AND THE
ALEX AFFAIR

Francis Durbridge

WILLIAMS & WHITING

Cover design by Timo Schroeder

9781915887238

Williams & Whiting (Publishers)
15 Chestnut Grove, Hurstpierpoint,
West Sussex, BN6 9SS

Titles by Francis Durbridge published by Williams & Whiting

1   The Scarf – tv serial
2   Paul Temple and the Curzon Case – radio serial
3   La Boutique – radio serial
4   The Broken Horseshoe – tv serial
5   Three Plays for Radio Volume 1
6   Send for Paul Temple – radio serial
7   A Time of Day – tv serial
8   Death Comes to The Hibiscus – stage play
    The Essential Heart – radio play
    (writing as Nicholas Vane)
9   Send for Paul Temple – stage play
10 The Teckman Biography – tv serial
11 Paul Temple and Steve – radio serial
12 Twenty Minutes From Rome – a teleplay
13 Portrait of Alison – tv serial
14 Paul Temple: Two Plays for Radio Volume 1
15 Three Plays for Radio Volume 2
16 The Other Man – tv serial
17 Paul Temple and the Spencer Affair – radio serial
18 Step In The Dark – film script
19 My Friend Charles – tv serial
20 A Case For Paul Temple – radio serial
21 Murder In The Media – more rediscovered serials and
    stories
22 The Desperate People – tv serial
23 Paul Temple: Two Plays for Television
24 And Anthony Sherwood Laughed – radio series
25 The World of Tim Frazer – tv serial
26 Paul Temple Intervenes – radio serial
27 Passport To Danger! – radio serial
28 Bat Out of Hell – tv serial
29 Send For Paul Temple Again – radio serial

Murder At The Weekend – the rediscovered newspaper serials and short stories

Also published by Williams & Whiting:

Francis Durbridge: The Complete Guide
By Melvyn Barnes

Titles by Francis Durbridge to be published by Williams & Whiting
Kind Regards From Mr Brix – a magazine serial
Paul Temple and the Canterbury Case (film script)
Paul Temple: Two Plays For Radio Vol 2 (Send For Paul Temple and News of Paul Temple)
The Face of Carol West – a magazine serial
The Yellow Windmill – a magazine serial

INTRODUCTION

Francis Durbridge's *Paul Temple and the Alex Affair* (1968) is often described as the last Paul Temple radio serial, but this is only chronologically correct. Its origin was his 1945 radio serial *Send for Paul Temple Again*, which was given a new lease of life twenty-three years later after Durbridge had been pressed to write a new Paul Temple serial to follow *Paul Temple and the Geneva Mystery* (1965).

Paul Temple and the Alex Affair was broadcast from 26 February to 21 March 1968, with its eight thirty-minute episodes broadcast unusually in two episodes per week. It was Durbridge's re-writing of *Send for Paul Temple Again*, and this new version had Peter Coke as Temple for the eleventh time and Marjorie Westbury as Steve for the twenty-second time. The villain's sobriquet became Alex rather than Rex, the original episode titles were replaced, and there were other updates and revisions. Furthermore the eventual broadcast had several changes of structure, scenes and dialogue when compared with Durbridge's original script as published in this volume – and as witness, the recorded serial was marketed in audiocassettes and CDs (BBC Audio, 2003) and also included in the CD set *Paul Temple : The Complete Radio Collection: The Sixties 1960-1968* (BBC, 2017).

Alex was the final radio work of Francis Durbridge (1912-98), who had begun in 1933 as a prolific writer of sketches, stories and plays for BBC radio. They were mostly light entertainments, but a talent for crime fiction became evident in his early radio plays *Murder in the Midlands* (1934) and *Murder in the Embassy* (1937). Then in 1938 he had the brainwave that was to define his career.

Durbridge's radio dream team of novelist/detective Paul Temple and his wife Steve, who first appeared in the serial

Send for Paul Temple (8 April to 27 May 1938), attracted over 7,000 fan letters that resulted in a succession of twenty more Temple cases plus new productions of seven of them. And Paul Temple in the mid-twentieth century saw him vie with radio rivals including Dick Barton (by Edward J. Mason), Philip Odell (by Lester Powell), Dr. Morelle (by Ernest Dudley), P.C. 49 (by Alan Stranks) and Ambrose West (by Philip Levene).

The Paul Temple serials soon acquired an enormous European following, with translated versions broadcast in the Netherlands from 1939, Germany from 1949, Italy from 1953 and Denmark from 1954. In the case of *Paul Temple and the Alex Affair*, the German radio version *Paul Temple und der Fall Alex* (16 February – 5 April 1968, eight episodes) was translated by Marianne de Barde and produced by Otto Düben, with Paul Klinger as Temple and Margot Leonhardt as Steve; the Dutch radio version *Paul Vlaanderen en het Alex mysterie* (7 January – 25 February 1969, eight episodes) was translated by Alfred Pleiter and produced by Dick van Putten, with Johan Schmitz as Vlaanderen and Wieke Mulier as Ina; and among other translations it was broadcast on Radio Israel.

Then in 1952, while continuing to write for radio, Durbridge embarked on a long sequence of BBC television thrillers that achieved enormous viewing figures. *The Broken Horseshoe* was the first thriller serial on UK television, and his many others included *Portrait of Alison, My Friend Charles, The Scarf, The World of Tim Frazer, Melissa, A Man Called Harry Brent* and *Bat out of Hell*. His popularity on the small screen was phenomenal, with the result that for all his serials from 1960 the BBC gave him the unprecedented accolade of the "Francis Durbridge Presents" screen credit before the title sequence of each episode.

Durbridge's radio career from 1933 until 1968 was overlapped by his television serials from 1952 to 1980 and overlapped again by his career as a stage dramatist from 1971 in the UK and even earlier in Germany. The latter saw a change of style from the "whodunit" form, and he became known for intriguing twist-after-twist plays including *Suddenly at Home, Murder with Love* and *House Guest*.

His radio serial *Paul Temple and the Alex Affair* had a long history. The original *Send for Paul Temple Again* was the fifth Paul Temple radio serial, broadcast from 13 September to 1 November 1945 in eight thirty-minute episodes. Then in April 1948 John Long published it as a novel, written jointly by Durbridge and Charles Hatton, and the UK audiobook was eventually marketed in a choice of audiocassettes and CDs, read by Peter Wickham (ISIS Audiobooks, 2008). One of the original 1945 radio serial's claims to distinction was that it marked the appearance of Marjorie Westbury (1905-89) as Steve Temple for the first of twenty-two occasions. And her co-star, for his only time as Paul Temple, was the Canadian (but London-born) actor Barry Morse (1918-2008). He also appeared the following year in Durbridge's radio play *The Caspary Affair*, but much later achieved worldwide television fame as the dogged Lt. Gerard in seemingly endless pursuit of David Janssen as Dr Richard Kimble in *The Fugitive* from 1963 to 1967.

Then given the hunger of mid-twentieth century cinemagoers for black-and-white crime dramas produced by British studios, it is not surprising that the Temples found their way to the silver screen. The film version of *Send for Paul Temple Again* was released by Butchers/Nettlefold in 1948, having gone through a succession of working titles as *Paul Temple and the Canterbury Case* and the prosaic *Paul Temple – 999* until settling for the final title *Calling Paul Temple*. The screenplay was credited to Durbridge and also to A.R. Rawlinson and Kathleen Butler, the producer was Ernest G. Roy and the director was Maclean Rogers. Many years later it was marketed on DVD (Renown Pictures, 2009) and was also included in the DVD box set of all four Temple films as *The Paul Temple Collection Limited Edition* (Renown Pictures, 2011). Most recently, *Calling Paul Temple* was revived on one DVD containing the English and German (dubbed) versions entitled *Wer ist Rex?* (Pidax, 2015).

Melvyn Barnes
Author of *Francis Durbridge: The Complete Guide* (Williams & Whiting, 2018)

This book reproduces Francis Durbridge's original script together with the list of characters and actors of the BBC programme on the dates mentioned, but the eventual broadcast might have edited Durbridge's script in respect of scenes, dialogue and character names.

PAUL TEMPLE
AND THE
ALEX AFFAIR

A serial in eight episodes
By FRANCIS DURBRIDGE
Broadcast on BBC Radio
26 February – 21 March 1968
CAST:

Paul Temple . . . . Peter Coke
Steve, his wife . . . . Marjorie Westbury
Sir Graham Forbes . . . . James Thomason
Inspector Crane . . . . Haydn Jones
Webb (Ticket Collector) . . . . Ronald Herdman
Wilfred Davis . . . . Basil Jones
Walter Day (Editor) . . . . .Anthony Viccars
Don Shaw (BBC Producer) . .Ronald Herdman
Donald Black . . . . .Victor Lucas
Sir Ernest Cranbury . . . . Geoffrey Wincott
A P Mulroy . . . . Michael Harbour
Lady Weyman . . . . .Betty Hardy
Lang .Anthony Viccars
Spider Williams . . . . Alan Dudley
Dot (Barmaid) . . . . .Hilda Schroder
Maid at Dr Kohima's . . . . Ann Murray
Carl Lathom . . . . Simon Lack
Mrs Trevelyan . . . . .Barbara Mitchell
Dr Kohima . . . . .Rolf Lefebvre
Ricky . . . . Frank Henderson
Sergeant . . . . .Duncan McIntyre
Bowker . . . . .Ronald Herdman
Frank Chester . . . . Nigel Clayton

Man . . . . LeRoy Lingwood
Sergeant Dixon . . . . Denis McCarthy
Telephone Operator . . . . . . .LeRoy Lingwood
Mrs Horne . . . . Betty Hardy
Bradley . . . . David Brierley
Sergeant . . . . Antony Viccars
Leo Brent . . . . Denys Hawthorne
Flora (Waitress) . . . . Rosalind Shanks
Cloakroom Girl . . . . .Rosalind Shanks
Taxi Driver . . . . Alan Dudley
Thomas, Hotel Clerk . . . . . .LeRoy Lingwood

EPISODE ONE

MRS TREVELYAN

OPEN TO: *The sound of a train rushing at tremendous speed through a tunnel.*

Gradually FADE DOWN.

A compartment door opens.

WEBB, the ticket collector, is calling at the various compartments.

WEBB: Tickets, please! … Thank you, sir! … Thank you, sir! … Tickets, please!

The ticket collector draws nearer and nearer.

He arrives.

A door slides open.

WEBB: Ticket, please, sir! (*Faintly amused*) Ticket, please, sir!!!

DAVIS: (*Suddenly, waking up*) Oh!

WEBB chuckles.

WILFRED DAVIS is a young man of about twenty-seven or eight. He has a very pronounced Welsh accent.

WEBB: Sorry to wake you, sir.

DAVIS: (*Sleepy, but not unpleasant*) Oh – oh, that's all right. Lordy, I was hard on! (*Yawning*) What time is it now?

WEBB: It's half past ten, sir.

DAVIS: Oh. About another half an hour before we reach London?

WEBB: Yes, sir.

DAVIS: Not many people travelling tonight …

WEBB: Haven't 'ad it as quiet as this for months – train's half empty. (*He clips DAVIS' ticket*) Thank you. Goodnight.

The door closes.

Pause.

The sound of the train.

Another compartment door opens.

3

WEBB: Ticket, please, miss. (*Raising his voice*) Ticket, please! (*A moment: to himself*) Cor' blimey! (*Raising his voice: authoritatively*) Come along, miss! Wake up! Ticket, please! Come along, miss! (*Shaking her*) Come along! Wake up! Your ticket if you … (*Suddenly, staggered*) Strewth!!!

The door is pushed open.

A moment.

A second door opens.

DAVIS: (*Surprised*) What is it, man, have you seen a ghost or something?

WEBB: (*Nervously*) Would you mind coming into the next compartment, sir – it's – it's a young lady, sir – I – I – I think she's been taken ill.

DAVIS: Why, yes, of course!

A moment.

The sound of the train.

FADE train.

WEBB: (*Anxiously*) What is it? What's the matter with her?

DAVIS: (*Aghast*) What's the matter with her? Why, man, she's dead!

WEBB: D-dead! (*Suddenly*) Look in the corner … Looks what's chalked on the window … (*Breathlessly, stunned*) What – what does it say?

DAVIS: A – L – E – X (*A moment*) Alex! Now what does that mean, I wonder …?

FADE UP of music.

FADE DOWN of music.

FADE UP an Editorial Room of the London Graphic.

FADE UP the voice of WALTER DAY.

WALTER: (*Banging a telephone receiver impatiently*) Hello! … Hello! … What the hell are they doing? … Oh, hello – is that you George? … Listen! … I've just seen your copy on the ALEX murder, and it stinks! … Well, to start with, I want an entirely new heading! SCOTLAND-YARD-SENDS-FOR-PAUL-TEMPLE! (*Angrily*) Of course they have! Damn it, man, it sticks out a mile! Forbes left the Yard an hour ago – he's with Temple now … What? (*Losing his temper*) Of course he's calling him in! What the blazes do you think they're doing!!!??? Drinking each other's health???!!!

Quick FADE UP of music.

Quick FADE DOWN.

FORBES: Well, your – er – very good health, Temple!

TEMPLE: Thank you, Sir Graham!

CRANE: Good luck, sir!

TEMPLE: Skoal!

They drink.

FORBES: What on earth have you been doing with yourself during the past two or three months? I tried to telephone you about a fortnight ago, but …

TEMPLE: Steve and I have been staying down at Bramley Lodge. I'm writing a new novel – at least I'm trying to write one. It's supposed to be finished by the end of the month.

CRANE: I read your last novel!

TEMPLE: Oh, did you, Inspector?

FORBES: The detective was a bigger fool than ever!

5

TEMPLE: He had to be, Sir Graham, he was practically the Chief Commissioner.

They laugh.
A tiny pause.

FORBES: (*Quietly*) I suppose we don't have to tell you why – why we're here, Temple?

A pause.

TEMPLE: ALEX?

FORBES: Yes.

TEMPLE: I'm sorry, Sir Graham. I'd like to help you but – I've got this novel to finish by the end of the month …

FORBES: Temple, I don't think you realise just how serious this business is! It's damn serious! I saw the Home Secretary this morning and he asked me to deliver a message. He said: Tell Paul Temple …

TEMPLE: You tell the Home Secretary if he'll finish writing my novel, I'll catch ALEX for him! But seriously, Sir Graham – when did you first hear of ALEX?

CRANE: Oh – six months ago.

FORBES: Yes. A man called Richard East was murdered – he was found in his car on the Great North Road. Chalked on the windscreen of the car was the word … ALEX.

TEMPLE: I see. And that was the first time?

FORBES: Yes.

TEMPLE: How was East murdered, exactly?

FORBES: He was shot through the head, wasn't he, Crane?

CRANE: Yes, sir.

TEMPLE: Motive?

6

FORBES:	There didn't appear to be a motive. That's the extraordinary part about it, Temple! We just don't know what we're up against!
CRANE:	Well, it certainly wasn't money – East had about a hundred and fifty quid in his pocket when we found him.
TEMPLE:	M'm. And after the East murder?
CRANE:	Well, after the East murder we started the usual investigations, of course – without much success, I'm afraid. But we had no reason to suppose ALEX would strike again; not until the body of Norma Rice was found in a railway carriage, with the name scrawled across the window.
FORBES:	Yes, and there again, you see Temple, there didn't appear to be a motive!
TEMPLE:	Could it have been suicide?
CRANE:	Suicide? Miss Rice had just opened in a new play – it was a great success. Besides, she'd just got herself engaged to be married – everything in the garden was rosy. Couldn't possibly have been suicide, whichever way you look at it!
TEMPLE:	Was Miss Rice … shot through the head?
FORBES:	No! As a matter of fact when the ticket collector first found her he thought she was asleep.
CRANE:	She'd been poisoned – obviously someone had administered a delayed action poison. It was some while before it actually took effect …
TEMPLE:	And in each case the murderer left the name ALEX on a window?

7

FORBES:	Yes. On the window of the railway compartment and on the windscreen of the car.
TEMPLE:	I see. Tell me, is this word ALEX the only link between the two murders? The only reason for suspecting that they were committed by the same person?
FORBES:	Yes. Except that … (*He hesitates*)
TEMPLE:	Except that what …?
CRANE:	We found a card on Richard East – a visiting card. Written on the back of the card was the name Mrs Trevelyan.
TEMPLE:	Well?

A moment.

FORBES:	Go on, Crane …
CRANE:	Well, we found the same name in the back of a diary belonging to Norma Rice.
TEMPLE:	Mrs Trevelyan?
CRANE:	Yes, sir.
TEMPLE:	Oh. Oh, I see.
FORBES:	Temple, if I didn't think this business was serious then believe me I shouldn't …
TEMPLE:	Sir Graham, I'd like to help you! I'd really like to help you, but – well – you see, I made Steve a promise. I promised her faithfully that under no circumstance would I … (*He breaks off, then*) Sh! Here she is! Don't – don't say anything about this matter, please.

The door opens.

TEMPLE:	Hello, darling! Look who's here!
STEVE:	Sir Graham! After all this time! How are you?

FORBES: I'm fine! Gosh, you look younger every time we meet!

TEMPLE: Steve, what have you been doing to yourself?

STEVE: It's a new hat, darling – don't you like it?

TEMPLE: Is it back to front?

STEVE: Of course it's not back to front!

They all laugh.

FORBES: Oh – this is a colleague of mine, Steve. I don't think you've met.

CRANE: (*Turning on the charm*) No, but I feel quite sure that we've heard a great deal about each other.

TEMPLE: … Inspector Crane.

CRANE: How are you, Mrs Temple?

STEVE: How do you do, Inspector?

FORBES: Well, I suppose we'd better be trotting along. Thanks for the – sherry, Temple. Goodbye, Steve. I hope we'll meet again – pretty soon.

STEVE: Why don't you come to dinner one night. We'd love to have you – wouldn't we, darling?

TEMPLE: Of course!

FORBES: Thank you, Steve. I'll give you a ring. Say, one night next week?

TEMPLE: Splendid!

The door opens.

CRANE: Goodbye, Mrs Temple. I'm awfully pleased to have met you.

STEVE: Goodbye!

The door closes.

Pause.

The door opens.

TEMPLE:	Well – you look very pleased with yourself. Is it the new hat?
STEVE:	Yes. Don't you really like it?
TEMPLE:	It's stupendous! It's fabulous!!! (*Down to earth*) How much was it?
STEVE:	(*Laughing*) You are a beast! (*A moment*) What did Sir Graham want?
TEMPLE:	(*Lighting a cigarette*) M'm? Oh, he just happened to be passing and he thought he'd pop in – that's all.
STEVE:	(*A moment*) Paul, have you seen tonight's paper?
TEMPLE:	No, darling. Why?
STEVE:	Here it is. You see what it says …?
TEMPLE:	(*Reading*) "Scotland Yard Sends For Paul Temple". Oh, you don't want to take any notice of that sort of thing, why good gracious me, if …
STEVE:	(*Interrupting*) Paul, did – did Sir Graham mention this ALEX affair?
TEMPLE:	Oh, he mentioned it of course, in a general sort of way, but … Good Lord, is that the time? I say! I say, I must be off! I'm supposed to be at Broadcasting House at seven o'clock.
STEVE:	(*Quietly*) I'll drive you down.
TEMPLE:	Good! Then if you pick me up later we can have a spot of dinner together.
STEVE:	(*Still subdued*) Yes, all right.
TEMPLE:	(*Recognising STEVE's mood*) Steve, don't worry – I'm not going to get mixed up in anything! I promise you!
STEVE:	All right. And don't make a fool of yourself tonight!

10

TEMPLE: Why should I? Just because I'm in a discussion programme?

STEVE: Yes. But what will you do if they ask you some pretty awkward questions?

TEMPLE: I shall give them some pretty awkward answers!

STEVE laughs.
FADE IN of music.

FADE DOWN of music.
FADE UP of studio chatter. A little laughter.
About half-a-dozen people are present.

SHAW: Are you ready, old boy?

DONALD: No, I'm afraid we're not. Temple isn't here yet.

CRANBURY: I say, he's cutting it rather fine, isn't he?

DONALD: I'm afraid he is, Sir Ernest! Are the recording people ready?

SHAW: Yes, they're all set. Ah, here's Temple!

TEMPLE: (*Rather breathlessly*) I'm terribly sorry I'm late!

CRANBURY: You're not late! Not quite!

MULROY: Thirty seconds to spare!

DONALD: (*Raising his voice*) O.K., everybody!!! We're all ready now …

The chatter dies down.

SHAW: Now remember – although this is a recording – it's the real thing! So – so be on your toes …

LADY WEYMAN: Really – I've never felt so nervous!

A little laughter.

DONALD: Sh!

SHAW: Hello – Hello – Control room? … O.K.! … Yes, we're ready. (*A moment*) We're going

11

ahead in five seconds from … now …
(*There's dead silence for five seconds, then*)
We present Question Time, a spontaneous
discussion programme in which the panel
give their views on questions sent in by
listeners. We have with us in the studio this
evening A.P. Mulroy – Editor of The
London Tribune – Sir Ernest Cranbury,
Professor of Economics at Preston
University, Paul Temple – novelist and
private investigator – Lady Weyman – and
Dr Howard Lang, Principal of Rexton
University. The question master is Donald
Black.

DONALD: Well, our first question this evening comes
from Mrs Palfrey of Chorley Forest,
Abingdale, near Brentwood. Mrs Palfrey
asks the panel what is meant by the
'Science' of a particular subject. Is it
correct, she says, for instance, to speak of –
the Science of History …?

A moment.
LADY WEYMAN gives a nervous little laugh.

DONALD: Dr Lang?

LANG: Well, of course, it depends what you mean
by the word 'Science'. If one takes it
literally then obviously the only intelligent
…

*As LANG speaks SIR ERNEST CARBURY falls forward
across the table and the carafe of water smashes to the
floor.*
LADY WEYMAN gives a little scream.

LADY WEYMAN: Oh!

MULROY: Sir Ernest!

12

LADY WEYMAN:	What's – the – matter?
CRANBURY:	It's – it's my heart, I can feel it … feel it racing …
SHAW:	Hello, Control Room! Hold on! There's been an accident here!
LADY WEYMAN:	Sir Ernest, are you all right?
CRANBURY:	Yes, I … I'll be all right, I … I say, I'm most terribly sorry about all this …
DONALD:	Nonsense! Get some water somebody …
TEMPLE:	No, don't try and get up, Sir Ernest.
CRANBURY:	Oh, but I must, I can't stay … (*He gives another little cry of pain*)
TEMPLE:	Now take it easy, sir – don't excite yourself.
CRANBURY:	Temple, listen! There's something I want you to know, just in case … something happens …
TEMPLE:	Nothing's going to happen, you'll be all right!
MULROY:	Of course! It's just a nasty turn – we all get this sort of thing.
CRANBURY:	(*Rather desperately*) No! No, it isn't, you see … Temple, listen! I … I want to tell you about … about ALEX!
TEMPLE:	About ALEX …?

There is a general murmur of astonishment.

MULROY:	ALEX!
CRANBURY:	Yes … Now listen … When I first received … the letter I … (*Suddenly, he gives a quick little cry*)

There is a momentary pause.

MULROY:	Temple!
LADY WEYMAN:	Oh! Oh, is he …

13

TEMPLE: He's dead!
FADE UP of music.

FADE DOWN of music.
FADE UP the sound of a car.
It is cruising along at an average speed.

STEVE: Was Sir Ernest married?

TEMPLE: No – he was a bachelor. Lived in a service flat just off Park Lane.

STEVE: It must have been a dreadful shock to everybody in the studio.

TEMPLE: It certainly was! We didn't know what on earth to do!

STEVE: What did the doctor say when he arrived?

TEMPLE: There was nothing he could say. Heart failure – over excitement. There'll be an inquest of course.

A tiny pause.

STEVE: Do you think it was heart failure – just over excitement?

TEMPLE: (*After a pause*) No.

STEVE: What did Sir Ernest mean when he said "I want to tell you about ALEX"?

TEMPLE: I don't know. I've been thinking about it ever since. There was something else too – something else which rather intrigued me.

STEVE: What?

TEMPLE: Well – we had to search his pockets. As a matter of fact we were trying to find his address. Inside his wallet there was a small piece of paper – it dropped on to the floor. No one else noticed it so I – er – (*With an uneasy little laugh*) Well – here it is …

STEVE: (*A moment*) There's nothing on this, Paul.

14

TEMPLE: Yes, in the corner – in pencil.

The sound of a second car approaching can be heard.

STEVE: Oh! (*Reading*) "Mrs Trevelyan". Why, that was the name you told me about! The name they found on the visiting card and in the diary belonging to Norma Rice…

TEMPLE: Yes.

STEVE: But Paul, I don't understand! Why on earth should … (*Change of tone, almost an aside*) Darling, do pull over, that car is trying to pass us …

The second car commences to overtake them.

TEMPLE: By Timothy, he seems to be in a hurry!

STEVE: Pull over, dear!

TEMPLE: What the devil is he trying to do?!

STEVE: He's forcing me over!

There is the sound of a sudden screeching of brakes – and quick acceleration of the second car making its getaway.

STEVE: (*Breathlessly*) He nearly forced us into that shop window.

TEMPLE: Yes, and it was done deliberately – there's no doubt about that, Steve.

STEVE: No.

TEMPLE: Did you see the man who was driving …?

STEVE: No, I didn't.

TEMPLE: I didn't either – unfortunately. But I got the number. DVC …

STEVE: DVC 629 …

TEMPLE: Yes …

STEVE: I suppose you could trace it – the number, I mean?

TEMPLE: Yes, of course – if it's genuine, but …

STEVE: But what …?

TEMPLE:	Well, supposing this business has got something to do with ALEX?
STEVE:	With ALEX! But it can't have, Paul …
TEMPLE:	But supposing it has!!!!
STEVE:	Well?
TEMPLE:	Well – would you still want me to trace that number?

A pause.

STEVE:	Yes, I would! Forget that promise! Forget that promise, darling, if you really want to!
TEMPLE:	All right, Mrs Temple, if that's how you feel! (*A chuckle*) Hold on to that expensive hat of yours! Here we go!!!!

TEMPLE presses down the accelerator.
Quick FADE UP of music.

FADE DOWN of music.
FADE IN noises and chatter of a typical public house bar.

STEVE:	Paul, we've been waiting nearly an hour for this friend of yours!
TEMPLE:	Yes, but don't worry, Spider'll turn up all right. Have another pink gin!
STEVE:	No, thank you very much!
TEMPLE:	I take it you're not very impressed by this establishment?
STEVE:	Is one supposed to be impressed by it?
TEMPLE:	Of course! It's one of the most famous pubs in London!
STEVE:	Paul, what sort of a man is this – Spider Williams?
TEMPLE:	You'll soon see …
STEVE:	I can't understand you, darling! I really can't! Why didn't you get in touch with Sir Graham

about the car? Surely he could have found out …

TEMPLE: If I'm going to investigate this business I'm going to investigate it in my own sweet way! (*Suddenly*) Ah, here's our friend! Now don't laugh – he takes himself very seriously.

SPIDER WILLIAMS arrives.

He is a very nervous little man with a rapid manner of speech.

SPIDER: Hello, Mr Temple! Sorry I'm late, Mr Temple! 'Ad a terrible time getting 'ere. Terrible.

TEMPLE: Sit down, Spider. Oh – this is …

SPIDER: You don't 'ave to tell me who this is! Could spot 'er a mile off. Hello, Mrs Temple! Glad to know you. Sorry I'm late. 'Ad a terrible time getting 'ere. Terrible.

TEMPLE: Any luck, Spider?

SPIDER: Not a blaming thing, guv'nor. Not a blaming thing! I've 'ad Harris working on it as well and he's drawn a blank. Now tell me again – what sort of a car was it?

TEMPLE: I've told you! So far as I could see it looked like a Milford.

SPIDER: An' you say it 'appened last night just after …

TEMPLE: Just after nine o'clock. I'd left Broadcasting House and we were on our way down to Piccaddilly.

SPIDER: 'Course these cars aren't easy to trace! In the first place …

DOT: (*Cockney barmaid*) Is your name Williams?

SPIDER: That's right. What's up then?

DOT: You're wanted on the telephone – it's a Mr Harris.

SPIDER: Oh, thanks! (*To TEMPLE, quickly*) Hold on a
            jiff – he's perhaps discovered something!

SPIDER departs.

TEMPLE: (*Chuckling*) Well – what do you think of him?

STEVE: You have the nicest friends, darling.

DOT: Can I get you anything?

TEMPLE: Yes – the same again, please …

*WILFRED DAVIS arrives at the table and thumps TEMPLE
on the back.*

DAVIS: Why, hello, Simon! I never thought I should …
            (*He stops*) Lordy, you're not Simon!

TEMPLE: No, I'm rather afraid I'm not.

DAVIS: Oooh, now just fancy my slapping you on the
            back like that! Now what a stupid thing to do. I
            – I really don't know what to say, I …

TEMPLE: Oh, that's all right!

DAVIS: I could only see your back and I was sure that
            you were Simon Phipps.

TEMPLE: No, I'm afraid I'm not. My name's Temple.

DAVIS: Yes, of course, I recognise you now – Paul
            Temple. How very stupid of me …

STEVE: Mistakes will happen …

TEMPLE: Even in the best of families …

DAVIS: Well – it's very sporty of you to take it like
            that, I must say, but I feel an awful fool!
            (*Laughing*) Strangely enough I've only just
            finished reading one of your detective novels.

TEMPLE: Oh.

DAVIS: 'Murder on The Mayflower' …

TEMPLE: I hope you liked it.

DAVIS: Oh, it was most ingenious. Most ingenious.
            Mind you, I thought it was a bit obvious when
            that man jumped off the boat so suddenly. Of

18

	course, you know, I go in for that sort of thing a lot.
TEMPLE:	Jumping off boats?
DAVIS:	(*A little laugh*) Oh, no! Detective novels, I mean …
TEMPLE:	You write them?
DAVIS:	Mercy, no! I read them. Read them all day long. I've read four hundred and sixty-three detective novels in two years – that's really good going isn't it?
TEMPLE:	Yes, which ever way you look at it, that seems to be pretty good going!
DAVIS:	Anything to do with murder – crime – or criminology, I'm an absolute glutton. And yet, you know, I'm so docile myself. Couldn't hurt so much as a fly. (*Suddenly*) Ah, well – my profuse apologies, Mr Temple.
TEMPLE:	That's all right! Goodbye!
DAVIS:	(*Seriously, an afterthought*) Oh! If it's any consolation to you, my friend Simon Phipps is a very good-looking man. Goodnight, Mrs Temple!

A moment.

STEVE:	Goodbye. (*A moment*) Now what made him think I was Mrs Temple – you never introduced me?
TEMPLE:	You look like Mrs Temple. But what's more to the point, what made him think I was Simon Phipps? If he really did think I was Simon Phipps …
STEVE:	Here's Spider! He looks excited!
SPIDER:	(*Excitedly*) We've struck lucky, guv'nor. Harris struck oil, as you might say.
TEMPLE:	Well?

SPIDER:	That car: it was a six-cylinder Milford. Black. DVC 629. Had a GB plate on the back …
TEMPLE:	Yes, I think it had …
STEVE:	Who does it belong to?
SPIDER:	(*Chuckling*) D'you hear that, guv? Quite the little detective, isn't she? (*Seriously*) It belongs to a doctor, Mrs Temple. A Dr Kohima …
TEMPLE:	Dr Kohima …?
SPIDER:	That's right. Four ninety-seven Great Wigmore Street.
STEVE:	I think I've heard that name before. He's a Greek. A nerve specialist – a sort of psychiatrist …
TEMPLE:	Yes. Are you sure of this, Spider?
SPIDER:	We don't make mistakes in our business, Mr Temple – you know that!
TEMPLE:	Dr Kohima, you say?
SPIDER:	That's right.
TEMPLE:	Four ninety-seven Great Wigmore Street.

Quick FADE UP of music.
The music rises to a crescendo.

Quick FADE DOWN of music.

TEMPLE:	(*Reading the name on the brass plate*) "Dr Charles Kohima … Four hundred and ninety-seven" … Well, here we are, Steve.
STEVE:	Did you make an appointment?
TEMPLE:	Yes. I phoned through this morning. What are you going to do – wait for me in the car?
STEVE:	No, I noticed a registry office round the corner – I think I'll see if they can find us a replacement for Charlie.
TEMPLE:	That's not going to be easy. With all his faults I must confess I'm missing Charlie.

STEVE: I spoke to the doctor again this morning. It'll be another month at least before he's out of hospital.

TEMPLE: Well – see what you can do, darling. And remember I prefer brunettes.

STEVE: (*Laughing*) Yes, all right. There's no need to wait for me, Paul – I'll go straight home. See you later.

TEMPLE: Yes, all right dear.

TEMPLE rings the bell.

A moment.

He rings the bell again.

The door opens.

MAID: (*A young girl with a weak voice*) Good afternoon, sir.

TEMPLE: Good afternoon. I have an appointment with Dr Kohima – my name is Temple.

MAID: Oh, yes, sir. Will you come in?

TEMPLE: Thank you.

TEMPLE enters and the door closes.

A moment and then a second door opens.

MAID: Would you mind waiting in here a few moments, sir?

TEMPLE: Yes, certainly …

The door closes.

A pause.

CARL LATHOM speaks.

He is a man of about forty-five.

He is very well educated and has an extremely attractive voice.

CARL: (*Pleasantly*) Good afternoon.

TEMPLE: Good afternoon.

A pause.

CARL: Looks as if it's going to turn out nice again, doesn't it?

TEMPLE: Yes – I think it will – with a bit of luck.

Another slight pause.

CARL: Our friend seems to be as busy as ever.

TEMPLE: Our friend?

CARL: Dr Kohima.

TEMPLE: Oh.

CARL: Oh, forgive me! This is your first visit, perhaps?

TEMPLE: Well – yes – it is.

CARL: You won't regret it.

TEMPLE: I hope not.

CARL: A brilliant man. Really brilliant. Take my word for it.

TEMPLE: Haven't we met before somewhere?

CARL: I don't think so. My name is Lathom – Carl Lathom.

TEMPLE: Yes. I thought so. We have met about six or seven years ago at Lady Forester's.

CARL: (*He doesn't remember*) Oh? Indeed? I'm afraid I don't actually …

TEMPLE: Paul Temple.

CARL: Oh, yes, of course! You write detective novels and things …

TEMPLE: Chiefly detective novels …

CARL: Oh, please, forgive me, I didn't mean to be rude, I …

TEMPLE: Oh, that's all right. (*A moment*) If I remember correctly you once wrote a play …

CARL: Yes. (*Rather disinterested*) Had a very good run – made me a lot of money.

TEMPLE: Congratulations.

CARL: Oh – that's a long time ago.

22

TEMPLE:	Tell me, didn't a girl called Norma Rice play the lead?
CARL:	Yes, as a matter of fact she did. She was awfully good too. Awfully good. (*Suddenly*) I say, did you see that in the newspapers? She was apparently found dead in a railway carriage.
TEMPLE:	Yes. Most distressing business.
CARL:	Oh, most distressing. Such a charming girl too.
TEMPLE:	(*After a moment*) Have you written anything else since that …?
CARL:	Not a word. Not a single word. As a matter of fact I've been very ill during the past three or four years.
TEMPLE:	Oh, I'm sorry.
CARL:	I'm much better now – thank you.
TEMPLE:	Thanks to Dr Kohima?
CARL:	Entirely. He's really first class. He's such a – now how can one put it? He's such a well, quite frankly, such a personality. You feel instinctively that he's going to do the very best he can for you. (*A little laugh*) As you can imagine, that's rather important with a psychiatrist.
TEMPLE:	Yes.

A tiny pause.

CARL:	Will you have a cigarette?
TEMPLE:	Oh, thank you.

They light their cigarettes.

A tiny pause.

CARL:	Yes, I've been very groggy. Had one or two very nasty turns. (*A moment*) As a matter of fact, strictly between ourselves,

	I've been suffering from ... well ... (*A little laugh*) ...hallucinations.
TEMPLE:	(*Rather surprised*) Hallucinations?
CARL:	Yes. However I'm cured now – completely cured. But it was really rather – nasty while it lasted.
TEMPLE:	Yes, I should imagine so.
CARL:	I had the impression that everywhere I went I was being followed – and, oddly enough, always by the same person.
TEMPLE:	What sort of a person?
CARL:	A girl. Oh, a smart girl too. I could see her just as clearly as I can see you now. Brown shoes – brown costume – brown handbag – perky little hat! I suppose, really, it was quite the nicest type of hallucination.
TEMPLE:	And Dr Kohima convinced you ...
CARL:	He convinced me that she never existed, which, of course, she didn't. Oh, he's really quite brilliant.

The door suddenly opens and Dr Kohima's SECRETARY enters.

She is a woman of about thirty-five and is well spoken.

SECRETARY:	The doctor's sorry to keep you waiting, Mr Temple – he'll be able to see you in about five or ten minutes.
TEMPLE:	Thank you.
SECRETARY:	Your appointment wasn't till four o'clock, Mr Lathom – didn't you know that?
CARL:	Yes, but I found myself in the district with rather a lot of time on my hands so I naturally thought ...

SECRETARY:	Oh, it's quite all right, providing you don't mind waiting.
CARL:	Not at all.
SECRETARY:	I'll tell the doctor you're here.
CARL:	Thank you.

Door closes.

TEMPLE:	Was that Dr Kohima's secretary?
CARL:	Yes. An awfully nice person. Now what on earth do they call her? Oh, I remember! Mrs Trevelyan …

Quick and dramatic FADE UP of music.

END OF EPISODE ONE

EPISODE TWO

DR KOHIMA

OPEN TO:	*The door suddenly opens and Dr Kohima's SECRETARY enters. She is a woman of about thirty-five and is well spoken.*
SECRETARY:	The doctor's sorry to keep you waiting, Mr Temple – he'll be able to see you in about five or ten minutes.
TEMPLE:	Thank you.
SECRETARY:	(*A little surprised*) Your appointment wasn't till four o'clock, Mr Lathom – didn't you know that?
CARL:	(*Pleasantly*) Yes, but I found myself in the district with rather a lot of time on my hands so I naturally thought …
SECRETARY:	Oh, it's quite all right, providing you don't mind waiting.
CARL:	Not at all.
SECRETARY:	I'll tell the doctor you're here.
CARL:	Thank you.
Door closes.	
TEMPLE:	Was that Dr Kohima's secretary?
CARL:	Yes. An awfully nice person. Now what on earth do they call her? Oh, I remember! Mrs Trevelyan …
TEMPLE:	(*Obviously surprised*) Mrs Trevelyan …?
CARL:	(*Faintly amused*) Yes.
TEMPLE:	Are you sure?
CARL:	(*Laughing*) Of course I'm sure. (*A moment*) Why?
TEMPLE:	Oh. Oh, nothing …
CARL:	Mr Temple, I've been reading quite a lot in the newspapers recently about this person they call ALEX. Is it true what The London Graphic said last night?

29

TEMPLE: What did they say?

CARL: They said that Sir Graham Forbes had finally decided to – Send for Paul Temple.

TEMPLE: (*Quietly ignoring the question*) Are you interested in this ALEX affair?

CARL: Yes, as a matter of fact I am. I don't usually take an interest in murders and that sort of thing, but this business rather intrigues me. (*A self-conscious laugh*) I'm afraid I've even got quite a little theory of my own.

TEMPLE: What is your theory?

CARL: (*Laughing*) Oh, really! I've no wish to bore you.

TEMPLE: I'm not that easily bored, Mr Lathom.

CARL: Well, if you really want my opinion, I think that ALEX is nothing more or less than a … homicidal maniac.

TEMPLE: What makes you think that?

CARL: Look at the Norma Rice affair! What possible reason could anyone have for murdering Norma Rice? And then, take this business at Broadcasting House last night! Sir Ernest Cranbury. Now why on …

TEMPLE: How did you know about Sir Ernest?

CARL: How did I know? Why – it's in the papers! By the way, you were there! What happened exactly?

TEMPLE: Oh, Sir Ernest just collapsed – there was nothing very dramatic about it – it just appeared to be heart failure.

CARL: Then why are the newspapers saying that he was murdered by ALEX?

TEMPLE: Because Sir Ernest mentioned ALEX just before he died.

CARL: Did he, by Jove! (*Extremely interested*) What did he say?

TEMPLE: Oh, he simply said "Temple, I … want … to tell you about ALEX …"

A moment.

CARL: That was all?

TEMPLE: That was all …

CARL: Well, there you are! Obviously this ALEX fellow's a lunatic! Crazy as a hatter. Why should anyone want to murder poor old Ernest?

TEMPLE: You knew Sir Ernest?

CARL: Good Lord, yes! Oh, he wasn't exactly an old friend of mine, but we were quite well acquainted.

The door opens.

MRS TREVELYAN, the secretary, enters.

TREVELYAN: The doctor will see you now, Mr Temple.

TEMPLE: Oh, thank you.

CARL: We shall meet again, I hope.

TEMPLE: Yes, I – I hope so.

TREVELYAN: This way, sir.

The door closes.

TREVELYAN: (*Quickly; in a tense whisper*) Mr Temple, before you see Dr Kohima I've got to talk to you. I've got to talk to you about ALEX. Please believe me, it's desperately important!

TEMPLE: Well?

TREVELYAN: Come to this address – it's on this piece of paper. Come tonight, please!

TEMPLE: (*After a moment*) Tonight? At what time?

TREVELYAN: Half-past ten … You will come, won't you?

TEMPLE: Yes, I promise …

TREVELYAN: (*With almost a sigh of relief*) Thank you
               … (*Raising her voice*) This way, sir,
               please.

*MRS TREVELYAN opens a second door and in a voice free
from emotion announces.*

TREVELYAN: Mr Temple, Doctor …

The door closes.

*DR KOHIMA speaks: he is a Greek: a man of about fifty-
five.*

KOHIMA: Ah, Mr Temple! I am so very sorry to
               have kept you waiting. Do sit down, sir. (*A
               moment*) I received your telephone
               message this morning, from which, I
               understand, you wish to consult me on a
               purely personal matter.

TEMPLE: Yes. To be quite frank, Dr Kohima, I
               should simply like to ask you a few
               questions.

KOHIMA: This is not an interview – a newspaper
               interview?

TEMPLE: No, nothing like that.

KOHIMA: Then I shall be delighted! It will make a
               pleasant change. It is always I who ask the
               questions. However, I am at your service,
               sir.

TEMPLE: Have you a car, Doctor?

KOHIMA: (*Surprised*) A car? Why, yes!

TEMPLE: What make is it?

KOHIMA: It's a Milford. A six-cylinder Milford.

TEMPLE: Colour?

KOHIMA: Black.

TEMPLE: Registration number?

KOHIMA: DVC 629. (*Puzzled*) Why do you ask?

TEMPLE: Thank you. Now I'll tell you, quite simply,
             why I wanted to see you. At about a quarter
             past nine last night my wife and I left
             Broadcasting House and drove down to
             Piccadilly Circus. We'd just passed Oxford
             Street when suddenly a car drew level and
             made a deliberate attempt to force us into the
             nearest shop window. The car was a Milford.
             A six-cylinder Milford. Black. Registration
             number DVC 629 …

KOHIMA: But you must have been mistaken, Mr
             Temple! My car was not out of the garage last
             night!

TEMPLE: Where do you keep your car?

KOHIMA: Well, actually at my house in Regent's Park.
             But all this week it's been at a garage in
             Leicester Square – Sloan's Garage. I've been
             having certain repairs done, and – well – as a
             matter of fact I'm supposed to be picking the
             car up tonight. (*Suddenly*) Why don't you
             telephone the garage, Mr Temple, and verify
             my story? (*Quite pleasantly*) … Please, I wish
             you would. The number is Temple Bar 7178.

TEMPLE starts dialing.

TEMPLE: You've no objection?

KOHIMA: But of course not!

TEMPLE: Thank you.

A moment.

TEMPLE: Hello? … Who is that, please? … I'm
             speaking for Dr Kohima. The doctor would
             like to know if it would be convenient for him
             to pick his car up this evening? … Yes …
             Yes, a Milford, DVC 629 … (*A moment*) Oh
             … It was ready yesterday, you say? … I see

                              33

... Tell me – was it taken out of the garage last night? ... It was ... At about what time? ... Half-past seven ... And it was brought back at about a quarter to ten ... Who? ... Oh, yes. I see. Thank you.

TEMPLE replaces the receiver.

KOHIMA: (*Puzzled by what he has heard*) What did they say?

TEMPLE: (*Quietly*) The car was ready for you ... yesterday ...

KOHIMA: (*Surprised*) Yesterday ...?

TEMPLE: Yes. Also, it was apparently taken out of the garage last night.

KOHIMA: By whom?

TEMPLE: By your chauffeur ...

KOHIMA: What!

TEMPLE: He took the car out of the garage at about half-past seven and returned it – at about a quarter to ten.

KOHIMA: My – car – was – taken – out – of – the – garage – last – night – by – my – chauffeur??

TEMPLE: Yes.

KOHIMA: (*With a laugh*) Mr Temple, I'm afraid you're going to get rather a surprise, you see ...

TEMPLE: (*Completely matter-of-fact*) You haven't got a chauffeur? Yes ... I thought so ...

FADE IN of music.

FADE DOWN.

Suddenly, briskly, a door is opened.

RICKY: (*A Siamese: about thirty, very jolly*) Good afternoon! You are Mr Temple – yes?

TEMPLE: (*Taken aback*) Yes ...

RICKY: Welcome home, Mr Temple!

34

TEMPLE: Er – thanks very much.

Door closes.

RICKY: I'll take your hat and coat – thank you.

TEMPLE: Thank <u>you</u>.

RICKY: (*Unabashed*) Not at all. Swell day.

TEMPLE: Yes, it – er – Oh, hello, darling!

STEVE: Hello, Paul! (*To RICKY*) Oh, Ricky – this is Mr Temple.

RICKY: I recognised him. We get on pretty well together – I hope.

STEVE: Yes, well, er – that'll be all, Ricky, thank you.

A door opens and closes.

TEMPLE: Steve, where on earth did you pick him up?

STEVE: At the registry office. He's going to stay with us until Charlie gets out of hospital.

TEMPLE: Well – what is he? Siamese?

STEVE: Yes, and he's got awfully good references.

TEMPLE: All right. We'll give him a trial.

STEVE: (*Laughing*) Sir Graham's in the lounge …

TEMPLE: Oh, what does he want?

A door opens.

FORBES is talking to INSPECTOR CRANE and he stops as the door opens.

FORBES: Oh, hello, Temple!

TEMPLE: Hello, Sir Graham! Sorry to have kept you waiting. (*Pleasantly*) Good afternoon, Inspector.

CRANE: (*Not too friendly*) Afternoon.

FORBES: Temple, do you happen to know a man called Muller – Hans Muller?

TEMPLE: Hans Muller? (*A moment*) Yes – he's a Dutchman.

FORBES: That's right …

CRANE: (*Bluntly*) What d'you make of him?

TEMPLE: He's a crook.

FORBES: Yes, but …

CRANE: What sort of a crook?

TEMPLE: Oh, a fairly intelligent one … Why do you ask?

FORBES: We've received a letter from him, Temple, or rather the Inspector has …

CRANE: It arrived this morning – never having actually been in contact with Muller it rather surprised me.

TEMPLE: Do you mean the contents of the letter surprised you, Inspector, or the fact that you received it.

CRANE: Well, in a manner of speaking, both.

TEMPLE: M'm. (*Reading*) "Dear Inspector Crane, I am given to understand that you are personally in charge of the ALEX case. I would respectfully suggest, therefore, that you meet me tonight – shortly before midnight – at Granger's Wharf. I – know – the – identity – of – ALEX … Sincerely yours, Hans Muller."

STEVE: It sounds like a personal note from an old friend.

CRANE: I've never seen Muller – to be perfectly honest, I'd never even heard of him until this morning.

FORBES: We don't even know a great deal about him at the Yard, Steve. That's why I wanted to have a word with you, Temple. We know that he's a Dutchman and that he came over here about ten years ago, but that's all we do know.

TEMPLE: Pass me that book on the desk, Steve …

STEVE: Which one?

TEMPLE: The leather one. (*A moment*) Thanks …

FORBES: What's that, Temple?

TEMPLE: (*A little laugh*) Oh, it's a personal 'Who's Who'. I've been keeping this for years. Whenever I meet anyone interesting I always ... Ah! ... Here we are! ... Muller, Hans Muller ... born Amsterdam, 1910 ... M'm – speaks Dutch, Flemish, Danish, French and English. Hello, this is interesting ...

FORBES: What?

TEMPLE: Well, he's apparently very well off. He inherited quite legitimately – nearly a quarter of a million.

CRANE: Have you actually met him?

TEMPLE: Muller? Yes, I've met him twice. Once in Paris; once in the Hague. It's a good few years ago now, but ...

CRANE: Nevertheless, if you know this man, Mr Temple, it seems to me it might be a very good idea if you came along with us tonight. (*To FORBES*) What do you say, sir?

FORBES: Yes, by all means. All right, we'll – er – pick you up at about eleven. We're going by launch.

TEMPLE: (*Quickly*) No. I've an appointment at ten-thirty, so ...

STEVE: An appointment, darling?

TEMPLE: Yes, I'll tell you about it later. Where are you sailing from?

FORBES: North Pier ...

TEMPLE: O.K., I'll meet you at the North Pier, say ... eleven fifteen ...

FORBES: No later, Temple ...

TEMPLE: No later ...

FORBES: Right! Come along, Crane!

The door opens.

STEVE: Sir Graham and Inspector Crane are leaving, Ricky.

RICKY: O.K., Missie … This way, please …

FORBES: Goodbye, Steve! See you later, Temple!

CRANE: Goodbye, goodbye, Mrs Temple!

STEVE: Goodbye!

Door closes.

TEMPLE: I say, he'll have to stop that "O.K., Missie" business!

STEVE: (*Laughs, then*) Darling, what's this appointment you've got at ten-thirty?

TEMPLE: Yes, I was going to tell you about that. I saw Dr Kohima this afternoon and I had a chat to him about the car. It was his car last night, but – well …

STEVE: But what, Paul?

TEMPLE: (*Puzzled*) There's something very queer about the whole business …

STEVE: What do you mean?

TEMPLE: Well, in the first place, his car's in a garage in Leicester Square – being repaired. The doctor told me that the car would be ready for him today. But the garage people told me that the car was actually ready for him yesterday!

STEVE: Well?

TEMPLE: Well – his chauffeur is reported to have taken the car out of the garage last night at 7.30 and to have returned it at about 9.45 …

STEVE: Then, there you are! The accident happened …

TEMPLE: Yes, but you see, Dr Kohima hasn't got a chauffeur.

STEVE: But Paul surely – surely it's really quite simple! Someone pretended to be the doctor's chauffeur and …

TEMPLE: In which case, how did he get the car?

STEVE: How do you mean? They're pretty smart at that garage.

TEMPLE: There's only one way he could have got it. The gentleman in question produced a ticket and that ticket must have been the same ticket that was originally given to Dr Kohima.

STEVE: Oh. So that means that the Doctor was lying?

TEMPLE: Yes. But it doesn't mean that he drove the car – in fact I'm sure he didn't. And there's another interesting point, Steve. Dr Kohima has a secretary. A very charming secretary. Her – name – is – Mrs – Trevelyan.

STEVE: What! Darling, you're joking!

TEMPLE: No.

STEVE: (*After a moment*) Is your appointment – tonight – with – Mrs Trevelyan?

TEMPLE: Yes … She gave me this address and asked me to meet her there at ten-thirty.

STEVE: (*Reading*) "Forty-Nine A, Marshall House Terrace" … That's not far from here.

TEMPLE: No.

STEVE: Does Dr Kohima know about this appointment?

TEMPLE: No, and she seemed pretty anxious that he shouldn't know anything about it. (*Thoughtfully*) That woman's frightened, Steve. I don't know what she's frightened of – but she's as frightened as hell! Ah, well, I think I'll change. I feel like a bath!

Door opens.

STEVE: What is it, Ricky?

RICKY: (*Pleasantly*) So sorry. So sorry to interrupt – but – your bath is ready, sir.

TEMPLE: (*Surprised*) Oh. Oh, er – thank you very much. (*Suddenly*) No! No, just a minute! (*Suspiciously*) How did you know that I was thinking of having a bath?

RICKY: It is the duty of a good servant to anticipate the wishes of a good master. Sorry I interrupt … So sorry.

Door closes.

TEMPLE: Well, I'll be …

STEVE: Darling, he's going to be wonderful!!!

TEMPLE: (*Amused, yet nonplussed*) I don't believe it! I don't believe it!

STEVE: (*Imitating RICKY*) It is the duty of the good servant to …

TEMPLE: … to anticipate the wishes of the good master! In other words …

STEVE: You look as if you need a bath!

TEMPLE and STEVE both start laughing.

FADE IN of music.

FADE DOWN.

FADE UP of a bell ringing.

It is an old-fashioned (house) "Spring-pull" bell.

It rings for some little time.

STEVE: There's no one in, Paul.

TEMPLE: I'm not surprised. The place looks deserted.

STEVE: Are you sure this is the right address?

TEMPLE: Well, it's the address on the bit of paper, isn't it? Forty-nine A, Marshall House Terrace …

STEVE: Yes. Darling … The door doesn't seem to be locked, it …

The door opens.

TEMPLE: No, it isn't. She's probably expecting us to walk in!

STEVE: Paul, we can't just walk in as if …

TEMPLE: Don't be silly! We can always walk out again if we're not wanted.

The door opens and closes.

A moment.

We hear footsteps.

STEVE: The house seems deserted …

TEMPLE: Yes – but it's not empty. This room's pretty nicely furnished …

STEVE: (*Quietly, puzzled*) Do you suppose that she … lives … here?

TEMPLE: Mrs Trevelyan?

STEVE: Yes.

TEMPLE: Well, if she does she's very well off, because this place … (*He stops*)

STEVE: What is it?

A moment.

The ticking of a clock can be heard.

TEMPLE: Didn't you hear something?

STEVE: No.

TEMPLE: That's funny, I thought I … (*A little laugh*) I must have been mistaken.

STEVE: What are we going to do if she doesn't turn up?

TEMPLE: Oh, she'll turn up all right, she's almost bound to, unless … (*He hesitates*)

STEVE: Unless what?

TEMPLE: There's a suitcase over here, it looks to me as if someone's just arrived or … (*Suddenly, quickly*) Steve! Listen! Can't you hear something now?

A pause.

Only the ticking of the clock can be heard.

STEVE: What is it?

TEMPLE: Listen!

41

A second pause.

STEVE: Only the ticking of the clock …

TEMPLE: No! I don't mean that! Listen!

A moment, then quite softly, we hear the sound of a violin being played.

TEMPLE: Now do you hear it?

STEVE: Yes, it's a violin …

They listen to the music for a moment.

TEMPLE: I heard it before! I know damn well I'd heard it!

STEVE: But – but where's it coming from?

TEMPLE: It's coming from one of the bedrooms … Look here … You stay here, Steve, and I'll go upstairs and … (*He stops dead*)

STEVE: (*A moment; tensely*) Paul, what are you staring at?

TEMPLE: I'm just looking at the clock …

STEVE: Why, it's stopped!

TEMPLE: (*Slowly, thoughtfully*) It's been stopped all the time …

STEVE: But we can hear it! Listen!

TEMPLE: (*Suddenly, springing to life*) It isn't the clock, it's the suitcase!!!

STEVE: What are you going to do? Paul, don't touch it!!!

TEMPLE: Stand away from the window! Steve, stand away from the window!!!

TEMPLE picks up the suitcase and hurls it through the window, the smashing of glass is followed by an explosion. A moment follows during which we hear falling debris, etc. The violin continues faintly in the background.

TEMPLE: Thank God it landed on one of the flower beds! (*Almost amused*) It hasn't exactly improved the garden, has it?

STEVE: Darling, this is all beyond me …
TEMPLE: Come along, let's go back to the car …
STEVE: But Paul, what about the person upstairs – the person playing the violin? He's still playing.

The violin can be heard.

STEVE: Why, he's still …
TEMPLE: Yes. (*Decisively*) I'm going upstairs, Steve!
STEVE: I'm coming with you!

We hear the sound of footsteps running upstairs.
The violin grows louder.

STEVE: It's coming from that room, Paul – the door's open, but I can't see anyone …
TEMPLE: (*Quietly*) Just a minute, Steve! (*As he enters the room*) Well, I'm damned!
STEVE: Paul – what is it?
TEMPLE: (*Amused*) I don't think we'll find anyone up here, Steve.
STEVE: What do you mean?
TEMPLE: It's a record. An automatic record-player!
STEVE: But darling, why on earth should Mrs Trevelyan take the trouble to …
TEMPLE: I'll explain later! Come along, Steve – I've got to meet Sir Graham in twenty minutes.

They descend the stairs.

STEVE: Yes, all right. You can drop me on the corner, I'll walk from there.
TEMPLE: And when you get home you'd better tell that Chinese puzzle of ours to mix you a good stiff drink. You look as if you can use one!
STEVE: One!!!

TEMPLE and STEVE laugh.
FADE UP of music.

FADE DOWN of music.

FADE UP of the noise of a police motor-launch.

It is stationary: "chugging-over".

FORBES: How long will it take us to reach the wharf,
              Sergeant?

SERGEANT: (*Scots: a pleasant man of fifty-odd*) Oh,
              about a quarter of an hour, sir.

FORBES: (*Aside*) What time do you make it?

CRANE: It's gone eleven fifteen, that's a certainty!

SERGEANT: It's five and twenty past, sir.

FORBES: M'm. Well, we'll give Temple five more
              minutes and then if …

SERGEANT: Here's a car, sir.

The sound of a car is heard.

It draws to a standstill.

The car door opens and closes.

FORBES: Just in time, Temple! We nearly gave you
              up as a bad job!

TEMPLE: Sorry, Sir Graham! (*Pleasantly*) Hello,
              Sergeant! How are you keeping these days?

SERGEANT: I'm fine, thank you, sir. How's yourself
              now?

FORBES: You two know each other?

TEMPLE: We're old friends – aren't we, Sergeant?
              (*Politely*) Good evening, Inspector.

CRANE: Evening. (*Briskly*) All right, Sergeant! Let's
              get started!

*The SERGEANT revs up the motor and the launch leaves the
jetty.*

FADE DOWN of the police launch gathering speed.

FADE UP of the same launch out on the river.

*It is travelling very fast: there is a background of river
noises.*

FORBES: The mist seems to have cleared.

44

CRANE: Yes, thank goodness!

TEMPLE: Is that the place, over on the left?

SERGEANT: Yes, sir. That's Granger's Wharf.

A moment.

The launch begins to slow down.

TEMPLE: What sort of a place is this, Sergeant? Do you know it?

SERGEANT: It's just a typical wharf, sir. There's a warehouse, a landing stage, and a bit of a checking office.

CRANE: What's that place – the wooden shed – over on the right?

SERGEANT: It's the checking office, sir. I reckon if you've arranged to meet anyone that's where he'll be.

FORBES: Yes …

CRANE: Here we are!

The launch moves in to the side of the landing stage: TEMPLE jumps out.

TEMPLE: Throw me the rope, Sergeant!

SERGEANT: Here you are, sir.

A moment: the rope is tied.

TEMPLE: Right,Sir Graham! Give me your hand!

FORBES: Thank you, Temple.

SIR GRAHAM jumps on to the landing stage.

TEMPLE: All right, Inspector …?

CRANE: Yes. I'm all right.

CRANE climbs on to the landing stage.

CRANE: You wait here, Sergeant!

SERGEANT: Yes, sir.

CRANE: (*Staring around him; not impressed*) M'm …

TEMPLE: What are you looking for, Inspector, the reception committee?

45

CRANE: (*Not amused*) I'm looking for Muller, sir.

FORBES: Well, he doesn't appear to be here.

CRANE: No. The wharf looks deserted to me.

TEMPLE: Well, someone's been here, fairly recently too …

FORBES: How do you know, Temple?

CRANE: How do you … (*Suddenly*) Oh, the footprints – I've just spotted those.

TEMPLE: Yes. (*A moment*) Let's try that shed, Sir Graham. The Sergeant may be right.

We hear footsteps. Then they fade away.

A moment.

FADE UP of footsteps.

FORBES knocks on the wooden door of the shed.

CRANE: Well, there's nobody here by the sound of things!

FORBES: Obviously our friend Mr Muller got cold feet and changed his mind.

CRANE: (*Moving away*) There's a window over here, sir – but it seems to be partly boarded up. I'll see if I can …

TEMPLE: Just a minute!

FORBES: What is it?

TEMPLE: (*After a moment*) I think there's some paint or something on the door – you can feel it. Bring your light over here, Inspector.

CRANE: Right.

A moment.

FORBES: Great Lord, look!

CRANE: Look what's painted on the door!

FORBES: ALEX! (*Suddenly, tensely*) Temple, we've got to …

TEMPLE: (*Quickly*) Look out, I'm going to break the door
            down!

TEMPLE throws his full weight against the door.
It splinters, then gives way.

CRANE: My God, look at this fellow!!

FORBES: Look at his throat … Just look at his throat!

CRANE: Mr Temple, is this …

TEMPLE: (*Quietly*) Yes. It's Hans Muller …

FADE UP of music.

FADE DOWN.
FADE UP the sound of a key being inserted in the lock of a
front door.
The door is opened, then closed.

STEVE: Oh, hello, Paul! You're back earlier than I
            expected.

TEMPLE: Yes.

STEVE: You look tired, darling.

FORBES: It's not surprising! We've had quite a night!

STEVE: What happened? Did you see Muller?

CRANE: We saw him, Mrs Temple, but not quite under
            the circumstances we expected.

TEMPLE: He's dead. Murdered …

STEVE: Oh …

FORBES: Thank God you didn't see him ...

TEMPLE: (*Quietly, shrewdly*) You're looking pretty pale
            too! Did you get back all right, after you left
            me?

STEVE: Yes, but I had rather a … (*She hesitates*)

TEMPLE: Rather a what …? (*Suddenly*) Oh, it's all right,
            darling, you can talk. I've told Sir Graham
            about Mrs Trevelyan, Dr Kohima, and …

STEVE: Well, after I left you, Paul, I had rather an unusual experience. You see, I … (*She hesitates*)

TEMPLE: Go on.

STEVE: Well, I walked all the way home, as I said I was going to, but when I reached Curzon Street I had a strange sort of feeling that someone was following me all the time. I couldn't see anyone, and I couldn't even hear footsteps, and yet I felt sure that … Oh, it was most uncanny! (*A little laugh*) It – it was almost like an hallucination.

CRANE: (*Deliberately*) Well – perhaps it was an hallucination, Mrs Temple.

STEVE: Oh, no, it wasn't! Because you see, later – later I actually saw someone …

CRANE: You saw the person that was … following … you …?

STEVE: Yes.

CRANE: What was he like?

STEVE: Oh, it wasn't a 'he', Inspector. It was a girl.

TEMPLE: A girl! Are you sure?

STEVE: Yes, Paul, I could see her just as clearly as I can see you now.

TEMPLE: What sort of a girl?

STEVE: Oh, quite smart. Brown shoes – brown suit – brown handbag – perky little hat … silk stockings. (*A little laugh*) Quite smart, darling …

Quick and dramatic flourish of music.

END OF EPISODE TWO

EPISODE THREE

MR CARL LATHOM

OPEN TO: *FADE IN STEVE's voice.*

STEVE: … Well, I walked all the way home, as I said I was going to, but when I reached Curzon Street I had a strange sort of feeling that someone was following me all the time. I couldn't see anyone, and I couldn't even hear footsteps, and yet I felt sure that … Oh, it was most uncanny! (*A little laugh*) It – it was almost like an hallucination.

CRANE: (D*eliberately*) Well – perhaps it was an hallucination, Mrs Temple.

STEVE: Oh, no, it wasn't! Because you see, later – I actually saw someone …

CRANE: You saw the person that was … following … you …?

STEVE: Yes.

CRANE: What was he like?

STEVE: Oh, it wasn't a 'he', Inspector. It was a girl.

TEMPLE: A girl! Are you sure?

STEVE: Yes, Paul, I could see her just as clearly as I can see you now.

TEMPLE: What sort of a girl?

STEVE: Oh, quite smart. Brown shoes – brown suit – brown handbag – perky little hat … (*A little laugh*) Quite smart, darling …

TEMPLE: But this is extraordinary!

STEVE: (*Puzzled*) What do you mean?

CRANE: (W*atching him*) What do you mean, Mr Temple?

A moment.

FORBES: Do you know this girl?

TEMPLE: (*His thoughts elsewhere*) No.

FORBES: Then why are you so surprised that …

51

TEMPLE: Sir Graham, listen! When I went to Dr
            Kohima's this afternoon I met a man called
            Carl Lathom. Lathom told me that he'd been
            suffering from hallucinations. He told me that
            …

CRANE: (*An edge in his voice*) What sort of
            hallucinations?

TEMPLE: He was under the impression that everywhere
            he went – he was being followed. Followed by
            a girl, he said: "I could see her just as clearly as
            I can see you now. Brown shoes – brown suit –
            brown handbag – perky little hat …"

There's a gasp of astonishment from STEVE.

FORBES: I – don't – believe – it!!!!

CRANE: But that's fantastic!

TEMPLE: No, not when you really think about it,
            Inspector. It simply means that Dr Kohima was
            mistaken.

CRANE: Mistaken? About what?

TEMPLE: (*Faintly amused*) Well – about the
            hallucinations.

FORBES: (*Dogmatically*) Look here, you can say what
            you like about this business, but I've got a
            hunch that Mrs Trevelyan's behind all this. In
            fact, if you want my frank opinion, I think that
            …

TEMPLE: That Mrs Trevelyan is … ALEX?

FORBES: Yes.

CRANE: M'm – I don't know, sir.

STEVE: Well, she certainly prepared a nice little
            surprise for us tonight …

FORBES: Tonight?

TEMPLE: Yes. I had an appointment with Mrs Trevelyan
            at a house in Marshall House Terrace.

FORBES:	What time was that?
TEMPLE:	Oh – half past ten.
CRANE:	And what happened?
STEVE:	Instead of meeting Mrs Trevelyan we were introduced to a time-bomb!
FORBES:	Lord!
TEMPLE:	And not only a time-bomb, Sir Graham, but a rather ingenious little trick to keep us standing on top of it.
FORBES:	What do you mean, Temple?
TEMPLE:	Someone had fixed up an automatic record-player in one of the bedrooms, and …
FORBES:	A record-player? But why?
TEMPLE:	Because they knew that when we heard music we should …
CRANE:	You'd assume that the house was occupied and stand in the hall for a minute or two while the bomb exploded.
TEMPLE:	Yes, but how did you know that the time-bomb was in the hall?
CRANE:	In the hall? Did I say … in … the … hall?
TEMPLE:	Yes.
CRANE:	Why, I – I just guessed, that's all. (*A moment*) Was it in the hall?
TEMPLE:	Yes, it was in a suitcase.
FORBES:	Well, this settles one thing! I'll get a warrant out for Mrs Trevelyan tomorrow and …
TEMPLE:	No, don't do that, Sir Graham – not yet.
CRANE:	I think Temple's right, sir. It wouldn't be a very wise move to arrest her – not simply on a charge of attempted murder.
FORBES:	M'm. Where was the house, Temple – Marshall House Terrace, you say?
TEMPLE:	Yes, Forty-Nine A …

CRANE:	I expect we shall find details of the affair waiting for us at the Yard, Sir.
TEMPLE:	I'd like to see the report, if I may, Sir Graham?
FORBES:	Yes, of course. I'll phone you in the morning.
TEMPLE:	Thanks.
FORBES:	Are you ready, Crane?
CRANE:	Yes, sir. Goodnight, Mrs Temple.
STEVE:	Goodnight, Inspector.
FORBES:	Goodnight, Steve. No, don't trouble to see us out, Temple. We can find our way all right.
TEMPLE:	(*Moving away*) No trouble, Sir Graham. And if you could let me have details of the house – who it belongs to – who actually occupies it …

FADE SCENE.

FADE IN a door opening and closing.
A moment.

STEVE:	Paul …
TEMPLE:	(*Returning*) Yes, darling?
STEVE:	I don't think I care for that man very much …
TEMPLE:	Who? Crane?
STEVE:	Yes.
TEMPLE:	Oh, he's all right.
STEVE:	How long has he been at the Yard?
TEMPLE:	About six years. Why do you ask?
STEVE:	I wondered, that's all. He's probably just got an unfortunate manner.
TEMPLE:	Yes, that's one way of putting it. (*A moment; then suddenly*) What do you make of this business, Steve – this ALEX affair?
STEVE:	I don't know what to make of it! Sometimes, I think that ALEX must be – well – a sort of homicidal maniac. I mean, why should anyone

	want to murder Sir Ernest Cranbury, or Norma Rice?
TEMPLE:	Look for the motive.
STEVE:	But there doesn't appear to be a motive! Does there, darling?
TEMPLE:	(*Quietly*) No.
STEVE:	Well, I'm off to bed, if you …
TEMPLE:	(*Casually*) No. No, don't go for a moment or two – she'll be here in a minute, Steve.
STEVE:	(*Surprised*) Who?
TEMPLE:	Oh, didn't I tell you? Mrs Trevelyan.
STEVE:	Mrs – Mrs Trevelyan?
TEMPLE:	Yes.
STEVE:	(*Staggered*) She's – actually … coming … here?
TEMPLE:	Yes. At least, I shall be very surprised if she doesn't.
STEVE:	But, Paul, why should you think …
TEMPLE:	(*Quickly, seriously*) When Sir Graham and I arrived – with Inspector Crane – I noticed a car parked at the end of the mews. I'm pretty certain that Mrs Trevelyan was in that car …
STEVE:	(*Softly, excitedly*) A blue car with disc wheels and …
TEMPLE:	Yes.
STEVE:	Why, it was there when I arrived! (*Tensely*) She must have been expecting you then, she must have …

STEVE is interrupted by the flat buzzer.

A pause.

Then the buzzer sounds again.

| STEVE: | Ricky's in bed … |
| TEMPLE: | That's all right – I'll answer it. |

TEMPLE crosses to the door: the door opens.

MRS TREVELYAN speaks.

She is desperately on edge, near to tears.

TREVELYAN: Mr Temple, I've got to see you! May I come in?

TEMPLE: Yes, of course, Mrs Trevelyan. I've been expecting you …

The door closes.

STEVE: Good evening …

TREVELYAN: Good … evening … Mrs Temple.

TEMPLE: Would you like a drink?

TREVELYAN: No … no, I haven't a great deal of time, and (*Suddenly, tensely*) Mr Temple, would you mind drawing those curtains, please, I …

TEMPLE: No one can see you from the street, if that's what you're frightened of …

STEVE: It's all right, darling – I'll do it!

STEVE draws the curtains.

TREVELYAN: Thank you. (*A moment, then near to tears*) I'm most terribly sorry about what happened tonight … about what happened at Marshall House Terrace.

TEMPLE: It might have been worse. Not much worse, but – it might have been worse.

STEVE: Did you know that there was a time bomb in that suitcase?

TREVELYAN: (*Desperately*) No, I swear I didn't! I watched you both go into the house – I was at the bottom of the road. When the bomb exploded I … Oh, God, I didn't know what to do! (*She commences to cry*)

A moment.

TEMPLE: Mrs Trevelyan, I want you to listen very carefully to what I'm going to say. Some

56

months ago a man called Richard East was murdered – murdered by ALEX. A card was found on Richard East – a visiting card. Scribbled on the back of the card was the name Mrs Trevelyan.

TREVELYAN: No! I don't believe it!

TEMPLE: You remember the Norma Rice affair?

TREVELYAN: Why, yes! She was found murdered in a railway compartment.

TEMPLE: Scribbled in the back of a diary belonging to Norma Rice was the name Mrs Trevelyan.

TREVELYAN: (*Suddenly suspicious*) I don't believe it! You're lying! This is …

TEMPLE: I haven't finished yet, Mrs Trevelyan.

TREVELYAN: What do you mean?

TEMPLE: You see this piece of paper?

TREVELYAN: Yes …

TEMPLE: You see what it says?

TREVELYAN: It's got my name on it. (*Suddenly*) Where did you find it?

TEMPLE: On Sir Ernest Cranbury …

TREVELYAN: (*Weakly*) … Oh, my God!

STEVE: Paul, she's going to faint!

TREVELYAN: (T*rying to pull herself together*) No. No, I'll be all right, I …

TEMPLE: Let me get you a drink …

A moment.

TEMPLE mixes a drink.

TREVELYAN: I'm sorry, Mrs Temple – about tonight. Were you hurt at all?

STEVE: No.

TEMPLE: Here we are, drink this …

TREVELYAN: Thank you. (*She drinks*)

57

A moment.

TEMPLE: Is that better?

TREVELYAN: Yes, I feel much better … thank you …

TEMPLE: Sir Graham Forbes was here a little while ago with Inspector Crane. I don't know whether …

TREVELYAN: Yes, I saw them leave.

TEMPLE: Do you know Sir Graham?

TREVELYAN: Only by sight, we've never actually met.

TEMPLE: Sir Graham isn't a fool, not by any stretch of the imagination … (*He pauses*)

TREVELYAN: Well?

TEMPLE: Well, I thought you might be interested to know that he's under the impression that …

TREVELYAN: Well?

TEMPLE: Well, I thought that you might be interested to know that he's under the impression that …

TREVELYAN: That I'm ALEX?

TEMPLE: Yes.

TREVELYAN: (*Quietly*) Do you think I'm … ALEX, Mr Temple?

A pause.

TEMPLE: When I investigate a case, Mrs Trevelyan, I always make a point of trying to find out – right at the very beginning – what exactly it's all about. Sometimes that isn't quite so simple as it seems. Take this particular case for instance. Why did ALEX murder Richard East? Why did ALEX murder Norma Rice? Why did ALEX murder Sir Ernest Cranbury? There doesn't appear to have been a motive – but

58

	I'm quite sure there is a motive, Mrs Trevelyan – and I'm equally sure that you know what that motive is!
TREVELYAN:	(*A moment*) Yes, I know. (*Quietly, but still with a note of desperation*) Now listen: A few months ago I received a letter – it was signed ALEX. At first I thought it was some kind of a joke but I received a second letter and I knew then that … (*A moment's hesitation, then*) He demanded three thousand pounds. He said that if I didn't pay the three thousand pounds he would … reveal … a … certain … personal … secret … of … mine which …
STEVE:	What happened?
TEMPLE:	You paid the three thousand?
TREVELYAN:	Yes – but not at first. It was only after I read about the murder of Richard East that I decided to …
TEMPLE:	What do you mean – only after you read about Richard East?
TREVELYAN:	ALEX sent me a list – a list of names. Richard East was the first name on the list. I knew then …
STEVE:	You knew that … East was murdered … because he refused to be blackmailed?
TREVELYAN:	Yes …
TEMPLE:	Go on …
TREVELYAN:	I never heard another word from ALEX. Not until about three months later …
TEMPLE:	And then?
TREVELYAN:	I received a note. It was on my desk when I got to the office one morning. It simply said that he wanted certain information,

	information about a patient of Dr Kohima's.
TEMPLE:	I see.
STEVE:	And if you refused to give him that information then he …
TEMPLE:	(*Quickly*) Did you supply it?
TREVELYAN:	Yes.

A pause.

TEMPLE:	That's why you asked me to meet you tonight – you were told to do that, weren't you? Told to do it by … ALEX.
TREVELYAN:	Yes. The note was on my desk this morning when I arrived at the office …
TEMPLE:	Have you got that list, Mrs Trevelyan – the list of names?
TREVELYAN:	Yes, I brought it with me, and the note I received this morning.
TEMPLE:	(*Taking the paper, a moment*) Thank you.
STEVE:	(*After a tiny pause*) Paul – Paul, the first four names are the names of the people who have been murdered.
TEMPLE:	Yes.
TREVELYAN:	(*Tensely*) There are only three names left, only three names that …
TEMPLE:	(*Reading*) "James Barton … Norman Steele … and Mrs Trevelyan." M'm. This seems to indicate that Messrs Barton and Steele have followed in your footsteps, Mrs Trevelyan.
TREVELYAN:	I had no choice, Mr Temple, please – believe me.
TEMPLE:	You say that you obtained certain information about a patient of Dr

	Kohima's. How did you get that information to ALEX?
TREVELYAN:	I – I posted it.
TEMPLE:	Posted it? To?
TREVELYAN:	To the Waverley Hotel at Canterbury …
TEMPLE:	(*Intrigued*) Oh? Simply … to … the … Waverley Hotel, Canterbury?
TREVELYAN:	(*Hesitantly*) No, I addressed it to a Miss Judy Smith … those were my instructions.
TEMPLE:	Is that where – and how – you delivered the three thousand?
TREVELYAN:	Yes. I was told to make the money up into a small parcel and take it down to the hotel …
TEMPLE:	Addressed to Miss Smith?
TREVELYAN:	Yes.
TEMPLE:	Did you see anyone?
TREVELYAN:	No, I simply left it at the desk.
TEMPLE:	I see. (*A moment*) Tell me: how long have you been working for Dr Kohima?
TREVELYAN:	About six years. (*Suddenly*) Oh, please! Please – don't think that Dr Kohima's got anything to do with this. If he thought for one moment that I was mixed up in this business he'd …
TEMPLE:	I suppose you use a typewriter at the office, Mrs Trevelyan?
TREVELYAN:	Why, yes!
TEMPLE:	Do you know anything about typewriters?
TREVELYAN:	(*Somewhat surprised*) Well, I've used quite a few in my time I suppose and … (*Suddenly*) I can tell you one thing, Mr Temple – these notes, the notes I've received from ALEX …

61

TEMPLE:	Well?
TREVELYAN:	They've all been typed on the same machine.
TEMPLE:	How do you know?
TREVELYAN:	Well, if you look carefully you can see that the …
TEMPLE:	That the 'a' isn't very well formed, and there's a definite blur across the letter 'd' … yes. Could these notes have been typed on your machine – the one you use at the office?
TREVELYAN:	Good gracious, no! The notes have been typed on a portable typewriter and …
TEMPLE:	Hasn't Dr Kohima got a portable?
TREVELYAN:	(*Slightly bewildered*) Yes, he has, but I don't ever remember seeing him use it …
TEMPLE:	Well, I want you to use it, Mrs Trevelyan – tomorrow morning. I want a specimen of the writing of every letter on the machine! You understand?
TREVELYAN:	Yes, but …
TEMPLE:	I'll pick it up at about ten-thirty. If Dr Kohima should see me you can – er – you can tell him I'm still making inquiries about his car.
TREVELYAN:	(*Puzzled*) About his car?
TEMPLE:	He'll understand.
TREVELYAN:	But, Mr Temple, you surely don't suspect Dr Kohima! Why – why I've known him for ten years. He's a charming man. He's …
TEMPLE:	Mrs Trevelyan, in a case of this kind I make a point of suspecting everyone. Experience has taught me that a person

62

isn't necessarily innocent just because you happen to have known them for ten years, or just because they happen to be living with you or working under the same roof. In fact, in nine cases out of ten …

TEMPLE is interrupted by the sudden opening of the door. STEVE gives a momentary start of surprise.

A tiny pause, then TEMPLE says:

TEMPLE: What is it, Ricky?

RICKY: (*Apologetically*) So sorry I startled you, I …

STEVE: What is it, Ricky? I thought you were in bed?

RICKY: No. No, I was reading. I heard voices and thought perhaps you might like some coffee …

TEMPLE: Yes, that's a very good idea, Ricky.

RICKY: (*Pleased*) Thank you, sir.

TEMPLE: Oh, and – er – while I remember, Mrs Temple and I are probably going away for a day or so. You might sort out one or two things for me.

A pause.

RICKY: Yes, sir.

Another little pause.

RICKY: Coffee for three, sir?

TEMPLE: (*Quietly*) Yes, for three, Ricky …

FADE UP of music.

FADE DOWN of music.

A door bell is ringing. The door opens.

MAID: (*The young girl with a weak voice*) Good morning, sir.

63

TEMPLE: Good morning. Mrs Trevelyan's expecting me – my name is Temple.

MAID: Oh, yes, sir. This way, please, sir.

TEMPLE: Thank you.

TEMPLE enters and the door closes.

A moment and then a second door opens.

MAID: Would you mind waiting in here, sir, please.

TEMPLE: Thank you.

Door closes.

CARL: (*Pleasantly*) Why Mr Temple! This is a surprise!

TEMPLE: Oh, good morning, Mr Lathom.

CARL: I didn't expect to see you here – at least not at this time of the morning.

TEMPLE: (*Laughing*) I didn't expect to see you either if it comes to that.

CARL: No, I suppose not. (*A moment*) I – I have an appointment with Dr Kohima.

TEMPLE: I see.

CARL: I trust that you were suitably impressed yesterday, Mr Temple?

TEMPLE: Impressed?

CARL: With your consultation?

TEMPLE: Oh, yes. Yes, indeed.

CARL: A really remarkable man, Dr Kohima. Absolutely first class.

TEMPLE: I should imagine so.

CARL: He cured me of the most extraordinary hallucinations. I was under the impression that everywhere I went I was …

TEMPLE: You were being followed …?

CARL: Yes. (*Suddenly*) Oh, yes, of course! I told you, didn't I?

TEMPLE: Yes, you told me …

64

CARL: (*Laughing*) It really was extraordinary.

A slight pause.

TEMPLE: I don't suppose for one moment that it will, Mr Lathom, but if by any chance your hallucination returns …

CARL: (*Surprised*) Returns?

TEMPLE: (*Slowly, he is smiling*) I should advise you to consult me instead of Dr Kohima.

The door is thrown open and DR KOHIMA enters.

KOHIMA: Right you are, Mr Lathom! I'm ready for you now … (*Suddenly, surprised*) Why, good morning, Mr Temple! Have we an appointment?

TEMPLE: No. I called to see Mrs Trevelyan.

KOHIMA: Oh, indeed? (*Suddenly, dismissing LATHOM*) I'll be with you in a moment, Mr Lathom, if you will go into the consulting room.

CARL: Thank you. (*Pleasantly*) Goodbye, Mr Temple.

TEMPLE: Goodbye.

A door opens and closes.

KOHIMA: (*After a moment*) What exactly is it you – er – wish to see Mrs Trevelyan about …?

TEMPLE: (*Quite simply*) About your car, Dr Kohima.

KOHIMA: But I've told you all there is to tell you about my car!

TEMPLE: Yes, I know. But with your permission I should – I should like to have a chat with Mrs Trevelyan.

KOHIMA: (*Annoyed, but not showing it*) Very well. Just as you please.

The door opens.

KOHIMA: Ah! Mrs Trevelyan, this is Mr Temple. He would like to have a word with you.

TREVELYAN:	Yes, sir.
KOHIMA:	Satisfy his curiosity, Mrs Trevelyan – if you can. (*Suddenly*) Oh, and before I forget. I appear to have mislaid a pencil of mine – the silver one with my initials on it.
TREVELYAN:	It was on your desk last night, sir.
KOHIMA:	Yes – yes – I know it was on my desk last night but I haven't seen it this morning.
TREVELYAN:	I'll try and find it for you, sir.
KOHIMA:	I wish you would, my dear.

Door opens and closes.

A moment.

TEMPLE:	Well?
TREVELYAN:	I've – I've tested the portable. Here you are …
TEMPLE:	Thank you. (*A moment*) M'm. The typing isn't the same.
TREVELYAN:	No, of course not! I knew it wouldn't be.
TEMPLE:	Mrs Trevelyan, you took a risk last night in coming to my flat – you know that, don't you?
TREVELYAN:	Yes.
TEMPLE:	Well – take care of yourself. Watch your step.
TREVELYAN:	(*Nervously*) Why do you say that?
TEMPLE:	No particular reason, but – just take care of yourself.
TREVELYAN:	And what happens if I want to get in touch with you again?
TEMPLE:	You can ring me at … (*Taking out his wallet*) … this number.
TREVELYAN:	Thank you.

TEMPLE:	I shall be out of town tonight, but I shall be back first thing tomorrow morning. (*Casually*) In any case, I'm only going down to Canterbury …
TREVELYAN:	(*Surprised*) To Canterbury?
TEMPLE:	(*A little surprised by MRS TREVELYAN's reaction*) Yes, to the Waverley Hotel …

FADE UP of music.

FADE DOWN of music.
Slight background of chatter.

TEMPLE:	Good evening …
BOWKER:	(*An elderly waiter; bored with life*) Evening, sir.
TEMPLE:	We'd like a table for two, please.
BOWKER:	Are you staying here?
TEMPLE:	Yes.
BOWKER:	Oh. (*His tone implies that they have his sympathy*) Oh, very good, sir.
TEMPLE:	Come along, Steve!

TEMPLE and STEVE enter the dining room.

BOWKER:	This is the best I can do, I'm afraid.
TEMPLE:	That's all right.
STEVE:	(*Taking her seat*) Thank you.
BOWKER:	I'll be with you in a moment, sir.
TEMPLE:	He's making sure that everything's off the menu.
STEVE:	(*Laughing*) Who runs this place?
TEMPLE:	I think it's run by a man called Chester – he was in the office when I registered.
STEVE:	You didn't ask him about the mysterious Miss Smith?

TEMPLE: No, I'll have a chat to Mr Chester after we've sampled … Ah, here we are!

STEVE: Gosh, I'm hungry!

BOWKER: (*Dolefully*) Well – here's the menu, sir.

TEMPLE: M'm. (*Impressed*) Roast duck …

BOWKER: The duck's off, sir.

TEMPLE: Off colour or off the menu?

BOWKER: Both, sir.

STEVE: What about the roast lamb?

BOWKER: Oh, very tasty, while it lasted.

TEMPLE: But of course it's off?

BOWKER: Oh, yes, sir!

TEMPLE: Oh, yes … yes …

BOWKER: I might be able to do something in the fish line, sir – if you fancy a nice bit o' fish.

A pause.

TEMPLE doesn't reply.

STEVE: Fish, darling …

TEMPLE: (*His thoughts elsewhere*) What? Oh, yes! Yes – that'll do splendidly.

BOWKER: Very good, sir. (*Departing*) We'll do the best we can.

A pause.

STEVE: Paul, what were you staring at?

TEMPLE: M'm? Oh – oh, I was just looking at the menu, that's all.

STEVE: (*A little laugh*) There's nothing very remarkable about the menu, darling.

TEMPLE: Isn't there? Have a good look at it.

A pause.

STEVE: Well?

TEMPLE: Don't you think it's typed rather nicely?

STEVE: It's all right, I can't say I'm … (*Suddenly*) Why, Paul! The typewriter they typed this menu on is obviously … the machine that typed the notes – the notes that were sent to Mrs Trevelyan by ALEX.

TEMPLE: (*Deep in thought*) Yes …

STEVE: (*Suddenly, remembering*) Paul, I meant to ask you last night. Those two names, the only two names on the list, apart from Mrs Trevelyan, that …

TEMPLE: James Barton and Norman Steele?

STEVE: Yes. Had you ever heard of them before?

TEMPLE: I'd heard of James Barton. He's a director of Overland Airways and … Hello, look who's here!

WILFRED DAVIS arrives at the table.

DAVIS: (*Pleasantly*) Hello, Mr Temple! Now what are you doing in Canterbury? (*Amused*) Don't you remember me? We met the night before last – I mistook you for a friend of mine.

TEMPLE: Yes, I remember you, Mr …

DAVIS: Lordy, now I don't suppose I properly introduced myself. Davis is my name – Wilfred Davis.

STEVE: (*Laughing*) Are you still reading your detective novels, Mr Davis?

DAVIS: Just you try and stop me, Mrs Temple! I'm an absolute glutton for crime or criminology. (*Suddenly*) By the way, Mr Temple, this ALEX affair is a most extraordinary business, is it not? The newspapers seem to be full of the most gruesome details. Tell me, is it true that you are sort of – sort of – investigating the case?

TEMPLE: (*Non-committally*) Sort of, Mr Davis …

DAVIS: Well, now, that must be most interesting. Of course, naturally, I'm particularly interested in the ALEX affair.

TEMPLE: Oh? Why?

DAVIS: Well, you see, I suppose, in a manner of speaking, I'm almost part and parcel of it, as you might say. I was on that railway train, you know, when they found – when they found the body of Norma Rice.

TEMPLE: Oh, were you?

DAVIS: Yes. Actually, I was asleep in the next compartment.

TEMPLE: Did you see Miss Rice?

DAVIS: Lordy, yes. The ticket collector got excited and … dragged me into her compartment. My, it was a strange sight. She was kind of propped up in the corner, you know, and … scrawled across the window was the word ALEX.

TEMPLE: Yes … (*Complete change*) Do you often stay here, Mr Davis?

DAVIS: Oh, fairly frequently. I'm very fond of Canterbury. As a matter of fact I'm very fond of all these old – what you might call – historical places. Bath, Harrogate, York, Canterbury …

BOWKER returns.

BOWKER: (*Pushing past DAVIS*) Excuse me, sir …

DAVIS: (*Moving*) Oh, I'm sorry …

BOWKER: I've brought you some soup …

TEMPLE: Oh, thank you.

BOWKER: (*To DAVIS*) Is your name Temple?

DAVIS: No, this is Mr Temple.

TEMPLE: Yes?

BOWKER: Oh, well there's a call for you, sir. It's from London – a personal call.

TEMPLE: Oh. Excuse me, dear ...

BOWKER: You'll find the box in the corridor, sir. It's on the right.

TEMPLE: (*Departing*) Thank you.

Start to FADE AWAY from STEVE and DAVIS.

DAVIS: Are you staying down here long, Mrs Temple?

STEVE: No, I don't expect so. We shall probably drive back to London on ... (*Complete FADE*)

FADE SCENE completely.

FADE UP of TEMPLE lifting the telephone receiver in the callbox.

TEMPLE: Hello?

CRANE: Is that Paul Temple speaking?

TEMPLE: Yes.

CRANE: This is Inspector Crane, Mr Temple.

TEMPLE: (*Surprised*) Oh, hello, Inspector!

CRANE: I'm speaking for Sir Graham, sir, we tried to get you in London, but ...

TEMPLE: What is it? What's happened?

CRANE: Sir Graham would rather like you to come back to town, if you can manage it.

TEMPLE: Tonight?

CRANE: Yes – tonight.

TEMPLE: What's happened, Crane?

CRANE: There's been another murder. A man called Barton – James Barton.

TEMPLE: (*Pause*) Oh, I see. All right. Tell Sir Graham I'll come straight back to Town.

CRANE: Very good.

TEMPLE:	(*Suddenly, an afterthought*) Oh. Er – what happened to Barton – exactly?
CRANE:	He was shot.
TEMPLE:	Oh. (*Another tiny pause*) Did you find the revolver?
CRANE:	No. But I found something else … rather interesting …
TEMPLE:	Oh?
CRANE:	(*Rather pleased with himself*) I found it by the side of the body.
TEMPLE:	What was that?
CRANE:	A pencil! A silver pencil bearing the initials …
TEMPLE:	(*Interrupting CRANE*) C.K. …
CRANE:	(*Taken aback*) … Yes! (*A moment, surprised and faintly petulant*) You don't seem very surprised about the pencil, Mr Temple!
TEMPLE:	I should have been very surprised if you hadn't found it, Inspector!

FADE UP of closing music.

END OF EPISODE THREE

EPISODE FOUR

MR 'SPIDER' WILLIAMS

OPEN TO: *FADE IN TEMPLE's voice.*

TEMPLE: What's happened, Crane?

CRANE: There's been another murder. A man called Barton – James Barton.

TEMPLE: Oh, I see. All right. Tell Sir Graham I'll come straight back to Town.

CRANE: Very good.

TEMPLE: Oh. Er – what happened to Barton – exactly?

CRANE: He was shot.

TEMPLE: Oh. (*Another tiny pause*) Did you find the revolver?

CRANE: No. But I found something else … rather … interesting …

TEMPLE: Oh?

CRANE: (*Rather pleased with himself*) I found it by the side of the body.

TEMPLE: What?

CRANE: A pencil! A silver pencil bearing the initials …

TEMPLE: (*Interrupting*) C.K.

CRANE: (*Taken aback*) Yes! (*A moment, surprised and faintly petulant*) You don't seem very surprised about the pencil, Mr Temple!

TEMPLE: (*Smiling*) I should have been very surprised if you hadn't found it, Inspector!

CRANE: (*After a moment*) What do you mean? (*Faintly irritated*) What do you mean, you'd have been very surprised if I hadn't found it?

TEMPLE: (*With a little chuckle*) I'll see you at the house, Crane. Tell Sir Graham we should be back by half past ten.

CRANE: (*A moment*) Yes. All right, I'll tell him.

TEMPLE replaces the receiver and opens the callbox door. He bumps into FRANK CHESTER who is a man of about forty-five and has a slightly nervous manner.

75

TEMPLE: Oh, I'm sorry!

CHESTER: I beg your pardon!

TEMPLE: Oh, are you the manager?

CHESTER: Well – officially, yes. But just at the moment I seem to be the head-cook and bottle washer.

TEMPLE: My name is Temple.

CHESTER: Frank Chester. Anything I can do for you, Mr Temple?

TEMPLE: My wife and I arrived about half an hour ago but I'm rather afraid that we've got to go back to Town.

CHESTER: Tonight?

TEMPLE: Yes, I'm afraid so.

CHESTER: Oh, I'm sorry about that. I'll tell them at the office.

TEMPLE: Thank you.

CHESTER: Have you unpacked?

TEMPLE: No.

CHESTER: Oh, good.

TEMPLE: Oh, Mr Chester – a friend of mine stayed here a few months ago and I appear to have mislaid her address. I was just wondering if you could …

CHESTER: Yes, I can do that for you. When did she stay with us?

TEMPLE: Oh – it should be some time within the last six months. I can't recall the exact date, I'm afraid.

CHESTER: And the name?

TEMPLE: Smith. Miss Judy Smith.

A significant pause.

CHESTER: (*Nervously*) I'll – I'll do the best I can.

TEMPLE: (*Pleasantly; ignoring his nervousness*) Thank you. I shall be in the dining room.

FADE SCENE.

FADE UP of WILFRED DAVIS.

DAVIS: … and then we motored down to Naples, Mrs
             Temple, and I don't ever remember seeing a
             more glorious sight. You see, we … Ah! Ah,
             here's Mr Temple!

STEVE: (*Relieved*) Oh, yes …

TEMPLE: Sorry to have kept you waiting, darling.

STEVE: I should imagine your soup's stone-cold by
             now.

DAVIS: If I know anything about the Waverley it was
             probably stone-cold to start with! Well – I'll be
             off! Perhaps you'll join me later – for coffee?

STEVE: Well …

TEMPLE: I'm afraid not, Mr Davis – we're going back to
             Town.

DAVIS: Oh. (*Quietly, almost with a note of suspicion*)
             Oh, I thought you said that you were staying
             the night.

STEVE: (*Surprised*) Aren't we staying the night?

TEMPLE: No.

DAVIS: Oh, well – I'll be making a move. Nice to have
             seen you again anyway. Goodbye.

TEMPLE: Goodbye, Mr Davis.

A moment.

STEVE: What is it, Paul?

TEMPLE: I want to get back to Town as soon as we can.

STEVE: What's happened?

TEMPLE: It's James Barton. The man we were talking
             about. One of the names on the list.

STEVE: You don't mean that he's been murdered?

TEMPLE: Yes.

STEVE: But Paul, this is terrible! First Richard East, then Norma Rice, then … Oh, Paul, you've got to do something about this!

TEMPLE: Steve, listen – I'm putting my cigarette case on the table. When I give you the nod knock it on to the floor – you understand?

STEVE: But why?

TEMPLE: Do as I tell you, darling! (*A moment, then he raises his voice. Pleasantly*) Hello, Mr Chester!

CHESTER: Oh, here we are! Mr Temple, I'm terribly sorry; I've been through my books but I simply can't find any trace of your …

STEVE: (*Suddenly knocking a glass over, and the cigarette case*) Oh!

TEMPLE: Darling, do be careful!

STEVE: I'm sorry …

CHESTER: Allow me … (*He picks up the case*)

TEMPLE: Oh, thank you … oh, er – this is my wife.

CHESTER: How do you do, Mrs Temple? I'm awfully sorry that you've got to rush away like this.

STEVE: Yes, it is a nuisance – and I was so looking forward to staying the night in Canterbury.

TEMPLE: Business is business, my dear.

CHESTER: Of course! Oh, as I was saying, sir. I've been through my books but I simply can't find any trace of your friend, Miss – er … Smith. Are you sure that she did stay here?

TEMPLE: Well – I'm almost sure. (*Thoughtfully*) The Waverley. Yes, I'm sure she said the Waverley, unless of course, she said … the Wheatsheaf …

CHESTER: (*Laughing*) Well, in that case, I'm afraid I can't help you.

TEMPLE: No, of course not. I'm awfully sorry to have troubled you.

78

CHESTER: No trouble at all, sir. I'll tell them to get your car ready.

TEMPLE: Would you? Oh, thank you very much.

CHESTER: Goodbye, Mrs Temple.

STEVE: Goodbye.

A pause.

TEMPLE: Wrap the cigarette case up in your handkerchief and put it in your handbag …

STEVE: Yes, all right.

A long pause.

STEVE: Paul …

TEMPLE: Yes, Steve?

STEVE: Who is ALEX?

TEMPLE: Who is ALEX?

STEVE: Yes.

TEMPLE: Don't be silly! Ricky of course! Good heavens! Don't you read mystery stories? You can't have a mysterious Chinese floating around without …

STEVE: (*Laughing, in spite of herself*) Paul, I keep telling you he's not a Chinaman! He's a Siamese!

TEMPLE: Ah, well, there you are! He's not even a Chinaman!

STEVE: (*With a laugh*) You are a fool! (*A moment: seriously*) Aren't you really worried about this business, darling?

A tiny pause.

TEMPLE: Yes, I am, Steve. You know, it's like working on a gigantic jigsaw, Steve – with half the pieces missing and the picture torn to shreds. I keep asking myself the same questions over and over again … Why did Mrs Trevelyan really send us to that house in Marshall House

79

Terrace? If she paid ALEX three thousand pounds, then where exactly did she get the three thousand pounds from? Does Mr Carl Lathom really believe that he suffered from hallucinations? And if he didn't suffer from hallucinations then who's the girl in brown – the girl that followed him – the girl that followed you after we'd been to Marshall House Terrace? (*A pause*) And the pencil – the silver pencil belonging to Dr Kohima. Why should they find the pencil by the body of James Barton?

STEVE: Did they find it?

TEMPLE: Yes. And our Welsh friend, Mr Davis – Mr Wilfred Davis. Does he really spend <u>all</u> his time reading detective novels? Sometimes, I wonder …

STEVE: This case seems so complicated; I'm beginning to wonder whether we shall ever get to the bottom of it.

TEMPLE: (*A smile*) Don't worry – we will.

STEVE: But it's so full of surprises.

TEMPLE: Life's full of surprises, darling. Take this soup, for instance. It says tomato soup on the menu, and it looks like tomato soup. But does it taste of tomatoes? (*A moment whilst he tastes it*) Yes, it does! There you are, you see! Life's full of surprises!

STEVE gives a little laugh.
FADE UP of music.

FADE DOWN of music.
FADE UP of a car travelling along a country road.
STEVE: What time is it?

TEMPLE: (*Driving the car*) I should think it's about half past nine. What was the last place we went through – Faversham?

STEVE: Yes. (*A pause*) Did you speak to Sir Graham on the phone?

TEMPLE: No, it was Crane.

STEVE: I don't know quite what to make of Crane.

TEMPLE: He's got an unfortunate manner. You said so yourself, Steve.

STEVE: Yes, but it's not only his manner, he – well – he always seems to have such an air of mystery about him. I don't know what it is, but I always feel … that he might turn out …

TEMPLE: To be ALEX?

STEVE: Now, darling, don't be so stupid! He couldn't turn out to be ALEX, now could he? (*A moment*) Could he?

TEMPLE: (*Ignoring STEVE's question*) What do you think of Mrs Trevelyan, Steve?

STEVE: Why do you ask?

TEMPLE: I'd just like to know what you think of her.

STEVE: I think she's a woman with a past – in more senses than one. But I like her. I think there are times when she doesn't exactly tell the truth, but I've got a feeling that …(*She stops for a moment*) Slow down, darling …

The car slows down.

TEMPLE: Hello! What's the matter here?

STEVE: Looks as if the road's up or something …

TEMPLE: There's someone holding a lantern.

The car slows down to a standstill.

MAN: I beg your pardon, sir, but you'll have to make a detour – there's a bit of a hold up.

STEVE: What's happened?

81

MAN: There's been an accident, ma'am, further down
            the road – nothing serious but it's holding
            things up. Take the first lane on your right, sir –
            it's not much out of your way.
TEMPLE: The first on the right?
MAN: Yes, sir.
TEMPLE: (*Pressing down the accelerator*) Thank you.
The car gathers speed.
FADE OUT of the car.

FADE UP the car again.
STEVE: This seems a pretty long lane to me …
TEMPLE: We ought to be back on the main road by now,
            surely …
STEVE: I should have thought so …
Pause.
The car continues.
TEMPLE: It's very dark down here …
STEVE: Yes.
A moment's pause.
TEMPLE: I think I'll put the fog lamp on.
A click: a moment.
TEMPLE: That's better …
STEVE: Yes. (*Pause, then suddenly a gasp of surprise*)
            Paul, look! There's … something … stretching
            across the lane from that tree over there …
TEMPLE: My God, you're right!!! Get your head down!!!
            GET – YOUR – HEAD – DOWN!!!!
*There is the screeching of brakes, the swerving of the car,
and smashing of glass.*
The car rocks to a standstill.
The car engine stops.
TEMPLE: Are you all right, Steve?

STEVE: (*Quietly; getting her breath back*) Yes … yes, I'm all right. What – what happened?

TEMPLE: There's a wire rope stretching right across the lane – it's fastened to that tree over on the right. (*Slowly*) If you hadn't noticed it then …

STEVE: Oh, don't … (*A pause*) Paul, that rope must have been put there deliberately …

TEMPLE: Yes – quite deliberately. I'll turn the car round; we'd better get back on the main road.

STEVE: Yes.

TEMPLE: Are you sure you're feeling all right?

STEVE: I'm all right, darling.

TEMPLE: Good. Let's see if the car will start …

TEMPLE presses the starter: it whirs but the car doesn't start.

TEMPLE: M'm – not so good. I think perhaps I'd better … (*He stops talking*) What is it?

STEVE: (*Alarmed*) I – I thought I heard something …

TEMPLE: (*After a tiny pause: quietly*) Yes, so did I …

Silence.

Then a noise is heard, a strange, eerie noise.

STEVE: (*Alarmed*) Paul, what is it?

TEMPLE: (*Softly*) Sh!

Then as the noise is heard again, it can now be recognised as a man's voice.

He is obviously in great pain and is calling for help.

TEMPLE: (*Quickly*) Do you hear that?

STEVE: Yes! Where's it coming from?

TEMPLE: It seems to me to be near that tree. Give me the torch – it's in the side pocket. (*A moment*) Thanks. (*Slowly, flashing the torch*) Well, there's the rope, but I can't see anyone near the tree, unless … Good God!

STEVE: (*Horrified*) Paul, look! There's a man hanging from the tree …

TEMPLE: Wait here! Don't move from the car!

The car door opens and closes.

STEVE: Paul, I'm coming!

The car door opens again.

TEMPLE and STEVE push their way through the hedge.

The sound of the man groaning draws nearer and nearer …

STEVE: (*Horrified*) Oh, Paul … What are you going to do?

TEMPLE: I shall have to break that bough – it's the only way of getting him down. Hold the torch.

TEMPLE swings on the bough of the tree: it creaks then suddenly gives way.

The man falls.

TEMPLE: (*Breathlessly*) Go back to the car, Steve – you'll find a flask of brandy in the suitcase. Quick, darling!

STEVE: Paul, this is the man we met the other night! The man you spoke to about the car …

TEMPLE: Yes, so it is! It's Spider Williams. (*Quickly*) Get the brandy, Steve!

STEVE hurries away.

SPIDER: (*Weakly; but quite coherent*) I – I heard the car … I wondered what …

TEMPLE: (*Softly*) Take it easy, Spider.

SPIDER: (*Astounded*) Temple! It's – it's you, Mr Temple!

TEMPLE: What happened, Spider? Tell me what happened.

SPIDER: I … I did exactly what he told me, Mr Temple …I came down here with the money – and then at the last minute someone …

TEMPLE: What money, Spider? Who told you to come here?

SPIDER: Lord Stanwyck sent me. He had a letter – from ALEX – asking for four thousand pounds … It said …

TEMPLE: Yes, yes, go on … What did it say?

SPIDER: It said he was to meet ALEX here and hand over the money personally. But Stanwyck offered me two hundred quid if I'd bring it instead, and so I … (*He breaks off*)

STEVE is approaching.

SPIDER: (*Nervously*) Who's that?

TEMPLE: It's all right … it's only my wife …

SPIDER: (*Relieved*) Oh … (*Suddenly, rather excitedly*) Listen, Mr Temple. I saw ALEX! I saw ALEX! It … it …

STEVE arrives.

STEVE: Here's the brandy …

TEMPLE: Oh, good.

SPIDER: I'll be all right, Mr Temple, once I … can get on my feet!

TEMPLE: Yes. (*Unscrewing the flask*) Have a drink of this, Spider, and then we'll carry you down to the car.

SPIDER: Okay. (*With a sigh of relief*) Cor', I don't know why you turned up when you did, Mr Temple – but – but thank God you did.

TEMPLE: Drink this – then you'll feel better.

SPIDER: Ta. (*He drinks*)

There is a moment's pause, then SPIDER gives a sudden cry of anguish and drops the flask.

STEVE: Paul!!!!

TEMPLE: Good God!!!!

STEVE: He's dead! He's dead!

85

TEMPLE: (*Quickly; desperately*) The flask! Where is it?!!!! Where is it!!!! (*A pause; softly*) My God! Cyanide!

Quick flourish of music.
FADE UP of music.

Slow FADE DOWN of music.
CROSS FADE to the voices of SIR GRAHAM FORBES, INSPECTOR CRANE and TEMPLE.
SIR GRAHAM and CRANE are obviously in an argumentative mood.

FORBES: (*Raising his voice*) It's not a bit of use arguing, Crane! You can see what happened! You can see exactly what happened!

CRANE: (*Irritated*) We know what happened, sir, but the point is, what the devil are we going to do about it!

TEMPLE: (*Quietly*) There's only one thing we can do, Inspector.

CRANE: (*Turning on TEMPLE*) Oh, and what's that?

TEMPLE: Sit tight.

FORBES: (*Exasperated*) It's all very well saying "Sit tight", Temple – but you don't know what I'm up against here at Scotland Yard. I had the Home Secretary on the phone only half an hour ago and …

SIR GRAHAM is interrupted by the opening of the door.

FORBES: (*Annoyed*) What is it, Sergeant?

SERGEANT DIXON is an Irishman: about fifty.

DIXON: I heard that Mr Temple was here, sir, and I thought he might like to have the report on the cigarette case.

TEMPLE: Oh, yes! Any good, Sergeant?

DIXON: (*Pleased with himself*) You picked up a beauty, sir. A first- class print.

FORBES: Well, have you checked it?

DIXON: (*Unruffled*) To be sure we've checked it, sir! (*Faintly amused*) And what does the gentleman call himself, Mr Temple?

TEMPLE: He calls himself Chester – Frank Chester. He's the manager of the Waverley Hotel at Canterbury.

DIXON: Is he, now? Well, I'm blowed! An' they say that crime doesn't pay.

FORBES: (*Pulling DALY up; sharply*) Well, Sergeant?

DIXON: (*Respectfully*) His name's really Mulberry, sir. Michael David Richard Mulberry. He served a term for robbery with violence some years back, and he did a tidy little stretch for a similar offence before that.

CRANE: Well, there you are, Temple. You can see where the cyanide came from. Chester put it in the flask while you and Mrs Temple were having dinner.

FORBES: He felt sure that even if the trick with the rope didn't work you'd be pretty badly shaken and …

TEMPLE: And sample the brandy. (*Thoughtfully*) Yes …

CRANE: (*Quietly*) Sergeant …

DIXON: Yes, sir?

CRANE: (*Taking it for granted*) Get a warrant out for the arrest of Mulberry, alias Frank Chester …

TEMPLE: No, I wouldn't do that, Inspector, not … just … at the moment.

CRANE: (*Surprised*) Why not?

FORBES: Why not, Temple?

TEMPLE: Well, after all, Sir Graham, we're not really interested in Mulberry, are we? We're interested in ALEX.

CRANE: (*Irritatedly*) But supposing Mr Chester happens to be ALEX?

TEMPLE: That would be most intriguing.

CRANE: (*After a moment*) What do you mean?

TEMPLE: How can a man be in two places at the same time, Inspector? (*A slight pause*) As I told you last night, Lord Stanwyck was instructed to deliver the money to ALEX personally, but instead he sent Spider Williams.

CRANE: Yes.

TEMPLE: Well, when we found Spider ALEX had quite obviously just left him – but Steve and I had quite definitely left Chester at the Waverley Hotel.

CRANE: That doesn't mean anything. He might have passed you on the road.

TEMPLE: Yes, he might have – but he didn't! And there's another interesting point, Inspector.

CRANE: Well?

TEMPLE: Supposing Mr Chester – or Mulberry if you like – didn't put the cyanide in the flask?

FORBES: But he must have done! Who else could have done it?

TEMPLE: Davis.

FORBES: (*Slowly*) Yes. Davis. Yes, I never thought of that …

A buzzer is heard; a click and then a voice from a dictograph.

VOICE: There's a Dr Kohima to see you, sir.

FORBES: Thank you. I'll send the Sergeant down right away.

FORBES switches off the dictograph.

FORBES: Sergeant …

DIXON: Very good, sir.

A door opens and closes.

A moment.

TEMPLE: Did you send for Dr Kohima, Sir Graham?

CRANE: No, I did.

TEMPLE: Oh? Why, exactly?

CRANE: (*Bluntly*) Well, for one thing, I'd like to make sure about the pencil.

TEMPLE: (*Slightly amused*) You'd like to make sure that it really belongs to him?

CRANE: Yes.

TEMPLE: (*Pleasantly*) Didn't you believe me last night when I told you that …

CRANE: It isn't a question of not believing you, Mr Temple, it's just a question of …

TEMPLE: (*Pleasantly*) Making sure …

The door opens.

DIXON: Dr Kohima, sir.

FORBES: Thank you, Sergeant.

The door closes.

KOHIMA: Why, hello, Mr Temple! I didn't expect to see you here.

TEMPLE: Do you know Sir Graham … Inspector Crane?

KOHIMA: No, I don't think I've had the pleasure. How do you do, gentlemen?

FORBES: Do sit down, sir.

KOHIMA: Thank you.

CRANE: We're very sorry to drag you down to Scotland Yard, Doctor; but the fact of the matter is we're hoping that you might be of some service to us.

KOHIMA: Oh, this sounds interesting … Professionally?

FORBES: No, hardly professionally. You see …

89

CRANE: Doctor, have you recently lost a silver pencil – a silver pencil bearing your initials?

KOHIMA: (*Surprised*) Why, yes! You know I have, Mr Temple, you overheard me say so to my secretary, Mrs Trevelyan!

TEMPLE: Yes. But I didn't ask you the question, Doctor.

CRANE: When exactly did you lose the pencil, doctor?

KOHIMA: Well – I first realised that it had disappeared yesterday morning. I had it the day before that, I'm quite sure. But, Inspector, you surely didn't get me down to Scotland Yard just to talk to me about a pencil?

FORBES: Is this your pencil, Dr Kohima?

A pause.

KOHIMA: (*Quite calmly*) Why, no.

CRANE: It isn't?!!

KOHIMA: No.

FORBES: You're quite sure?!

KOHIMA: Quite sure.

TEMPLE: It's got your initials on it.

KOHIMA: Yes, so I observe. But it's not my pencil, Mr Temple.

FORBES: (*Bewildered*) You're absolutely sure that this isn't yours?

KOHIMA: Absolutely sure. (*Curiously*) Tell me: where did you find it?

CRANE: We found it beside the body of James Barton.

KOHIMA: Oh! Now I can understand your curiosity. (*A moment, slowly*) But it still isn't my pencil …

The telephone rings.
It continues for a moment.
FORBES lifts the receiver.

FORBES: (*On the phone*) Hello?

90

OPERATOR:	(*On the other end of the line*) There's a call for Mr Temple, sir.
FORBES:	Oh, thank you … It's for you, Temple.
TEMPLE:	Thank you.

TEMPLE takes the receiver.

TEMPLE:	*(On the phone)* Hello?
OPERATOR:	Mr Temple?
TEMPLE:	Yes.
OPERATOR:	Hold the line, please …
RICKY:	(*On the other end of the line*) Hello!
TEMPLE:	Oh, hello, Ricky!
RICKY:	So sorry to disturb you, sir, but there is a gentleman to see you. He says it is most important.
TEMPLE:	What's his name?
RICKY:	It's Mr Carl Lathom, sir.
TEMPLE:	Oh. (*A moment*) Is Mrs Temple in?
RICKY:	Not at the moment, sir.
TEMPLE:	All right – ask Mr Lathom to wait. I shan't be very long.

FADE UP of music.

FADE DOWN of music.
A door slowly opens.

RICKY:	Is there anything else I can get you, sir?
CARL:	(*Nervously, jumping*) Oh! No. No, I don't think so, thank you.
RICKY:	Perhaps another glass of sherry, sir?
CARL:	No, really, I'm quite all right.
RICKY:	Mr Temple should be here at any moment, sir.
CARL:	Thank you. (*Suddenly, with more self-confidence*) How long have you been with Mr Temple, Nicky?

91

RICKY: Ricky, sir.

CARL: I beg your pardon – Ricky.

RICKY: About forty-eight hours, sir.

CARL: (*With a little laugh*) Oh – you're pretty new to the job then?

RICKY: Very new, sir.

The door bell can be heard.

RICKY: Excuse me. I think that's Mr Temple.

A door opens.

A moment and then a second door opens and RICKY is heard talking to TEMPLE.

RICKY: Mr Lathom is in the lounge, sir. I took the liberty of asking him to have a glass of sherry.

TEMPLE: Oh, certainly, Ricky.

TEMPLE enters.

TEMPLE: Hello, Lathom! What seems to be the trouble?

CARL: Temple, I'm terribly sorry dragging you away from Scotland Yard like this but …

TEMPLE: That's all right! You didn't drag me away. Have a glass of sherry.

CARL: I've – I've just had one, thank you.

TEMPLE: Well, have another!

TEMPLE pours out the sherry.

A moment.

CARL: Thank you.

TEMPLE: (*After a pause; quietly*) You look worried.

CARL: I am worried, Temple. Desperately worried. I … well … I …

TEMPLE: Suppose you start your story at the beginning.

CARL: (*Rather tense*) At the beginning? If only I could! That's just the point, where is the beginning? Where is the … (*He pulls himself together*) I'm sorry. (*A moment, then:*) Yesterday morning – when I met you in Dr

92

Kohima's waiting room – you said rather a strange thing, Mr Temple. I haven't forgotten it. You said: "If by any chance your hallucination returns I should advise you to consult me instead of Dr Kohima."

TEMPLE: Did I say that, Mr Lathom?

CARL: Yes.

TEMPLE: Then I must have had a very good reason.

CARL: (*Tensely*) You don't think it is an hallucination, do you?

TEMPLE: (*Quietly*) Do you?

CARL: (*Suddenly, fiercely*) No, I don't! Every day – every night – everywhere I go, there's someone following me. I feel it! I feel instinctively that … That girl! The girl I told you about! The girl in brown! I saw her again last night. She followed me! She followed me from Hyde Park Corner to Shaftesbury Avenue. At first I couldn't believe my eyes. I thought I was seeing things. I just couldn't believe my eyes.

TEMPLE: You've never actually spoken to this girl?

CARL: Spoken to her! That's the extraordinary part about it! She disappears! She disappears like lightning. Last night I did my damnedest to try and …

LATHOM is interrupted by the telephone ringing.

TEMPLE: (*Quietly*) Excuse me.

TEMPLE lifts the receiver.

TEMPLE: *(On the phone)* Hello?

The sound of a callbox pay tone and a coin being inserted.

STEVE: (*On the other end of the line*) Hello, Paul?

TEMPLE: Hello, Steve! Where are you?

STEVE: (*Urgently*) Paul, listen!

TEMPLE: What is it? Is anything the matter?

93

STEVE: Paul, listen! I had an appointment at the hairdressers and …

TEMPLE: Yes, I know that …

STEVE: Well, when I left the house I had a funny sort of feeling again … that I was being followed.

TEMPLE: Go on, Steve …

STEVE: It was that girl, darling – the one that followed me the night we went to Marshall House Terrace. When I left the hairdressers, about ten minutes ago, she was still waiting for me. She's followed me here …

TEMPLE: Steve, where are you? Where are you speaking from?

STEVE: I'm in a telephone box in Harridges. She's waiting for me at the main entrance.

TEMPLE: Keep her waiting! Keep her waiting, Steve! I'll be there in five minutes.

TEMPLE bangs down the receiver.

TEMPLE: Get your hat, Mr Lathom, we've got a date!

CARL: (*Astonished*) A date?

TEMPLE: Yes! With an hallucination!

Quick FADE UP of music.

FADE DOWN of music.

FADE UP of a car drawing to a standstill.

STEVE: Paul, I'm terribly sorry, but she's gone. I was in the phone box … when …

TEMPLE: (*Disappointed*) Oh, Steve!

STEVE: I'm sorry, darling.

CARL: It's all right. You can see what happened, she … She obviously got wise to the fact that you were talking about her, Mrs Temple, and decided to make a dash for it.

TEMPLE: Yes. Oh, I'm sorry, dear! This is Mr Lathom.

STEVE: (*Recognising the name*) Oh!

CARL: Mrs Temple, what was this girl like? About twenty-eight or nine? Smart? Dressed in brown – brown handbag –brown hat …

STEVE: Yes.

CARL: It's the same girl all right. I'm hanged if I can make head or tail of this! I mean, why should she first of all follow me, and … and … then Mrs Temple?

TEMPLE: I don't know. (*Suddenly*) Jump in, Steve! We'll go back to the house.

The car door opens and closes.

CARL: No! My place is just round the corner. Come along and have some tea.

STEVE: (*A little laugh*) I could certainly do with a cup of tea.

CARL: Splendid!

The car starts to move away.

CARL: You take the first turning on the right and then continue until you reach …

FADE SCENE.

FADE UP of CARL's voice.

CARL: … Well, there you are, there's the story of my life. It's not particularly exciting, I'm afraid.

STEVE: I don't know. You seem to have had some very interesting experiences. How long were you in Cairo?

CARL: About eighteen months, that's all. I rather liked it – often thought of going back there.

TEMPLE: Why don't you?

CARL: Well – I really don't know. I suppose there's no particular reason why I shouldn't. Oh, do have another cup of tea, Mrs Temple.

TEMPLE: When did you leave Cairo, exactly?

CARL: Oh, it's quite some time since I was there … Let's see … Four or five years, perhaps. (*With a disarming laugh*) I say, you must think I'm a mysterious character! First of all I meet you at a psychiatrist's, then I tell you that I'm suffering from hallucinations, and now you learn that I've actually spent eighteen months in Cairo.

TEMPLE: Why shouldn't you spend eighteen months in Cairo? My wife actually spent two or three years there.

CARL: (*Pleasantly surprised*) Did you, Mrs Temple?

STEVE: Yes, but it was a very long time ago. Before I was married.

CARL: I must say, I rather liked it.

STEVE: Some more tea, darling?

TEMPLE: Oh, thank you. When did you write this play of yours, Lathom, the one that Norma Rice appeared in?

CARL: Oh, I wrote that thing ages ago. Shortly after leaving Oxford. (*Laughing*) No one was more surprised than I was when it clicked!

STEVE: Have you written anything since?

CARL: Not a word. I don't really consider myself a professional writer, Mrs Temple. I'm more of a sort of – well, a dilettante. I've a private income – and, well, quite frankly, I'm passionately fond of doing nothing.

STEVE: But you can't just do nothing all day long?

CARL: Oh, I don't know. I read a bit, play a spot of golf, knock around. I'm rather fond of travelling. Used to do an awful lot in the old days. Not abroad, I mean – just locally.

TEMPLE: Have you ever been to Canterbury?

CARL: Good heavens yes! It's quite a haunt of mine. Always stay at the Waverley.

TEMPLE: We had dinner there last night, as a matter of fact.

CARL: Did you, by Jove! A fellow called Chester runs the place – at least he used to. Don't know whether you met him or not?

TEMPLE: Yes, as a matter of fact I did.

CARL: Not a bad chap – always made me very comfortable.

TEMPLE: When did you stay there last?

CARL: At the Waverley? Oh, now you've asked me something! Must be almost a year ago, I should imagine. I got awfully tired of the food. I suppose they did their best, but you know what it is. I say, do have a cake, Temple, they're quite decent – my housekeeper made them.

TEMPLE: Thanks.

A tiny pause.

CARL: (*As if he's finally made up his mind*) Temple, there's something I've been meaning to ask you. I nearly asked you this afternoon, but …

CARL is interrupted by the door opening.

CARL: What is it, Mrs Horne?

MRS HORNE: I've brought you some more hot water.

CARL: Oh, thank you. Just put it on the trolley, will you?

MRS HORNE: And these letters have just arrived by the afternoon post, sir.

CARL: (*Taking the letters*) Oh, thank you.

A moment.

CARL: I say. These Income Tax people are optimistic, if nothing else!

STEVE laughs.

MRS HORNE: Is there anything else, sir?

CARL: M'm. (*Looking up*) Oh, no – no, not at the moment, Mrs Horne – thank you.

The door closes.

A moment.

TEMPLE: You were saying …

CARL: (*Opening a letter*) Oh, yes. I was saying, Temple – I intended to ask you this afternoon whether, in your opinion, this business with the girl is … (*He stops dead*)

TEMPLE: What is it?

STEVE: Is anything the matter, Mr Lathom?

CARL: (*Quite obviously shocked*) Temple, this letter! This letter that's just arrived.

TEMPLE: Well?

STEVE: What is it, Mr Lathom?

CARL: (*Softly; stunned*) My God …

TEMPLE: Lathom – what is it?

CARL: Read it … Here … Read the letter, Temple …

TEMPLE takes the letter.

A pause.

STEVE: What is it, Paul? What does it say?

CARL: Read it, Temple …

TEMPLE: It says … (*Reading*) Dear Lathom … If you are wise you will obey the following instructions. Next Tuesday evening drive your car down to the village of Haybourne, in Kent. On the north side of the village there is a small country lane known as Fallow End. Park your car at the point

98

where Fallow End joins the main Haybourne Road. Be there shortly after ten – ten fifteen at the latest. When you have parked the car walk back to the village; stay there until approximately eleven o'clock."

STEVE: But why? What's the point of all this?

TEMPLE: Wait a minute, Steve. I haven't finished reading the letter yet. (*Reading*) "Before leaving the car you will place on the back seat a case containing five thousand pounds. The money must be one pound notes – not numbered consecutively. If the money isn't in the car – or you fail to follow out these instructions – a letter will be forwarded to the press the very next day. This letter will explain in detail the precise reasons for your visit to Cairo in the Spring of 1963.

CARL: (*Softly; frightened*) Oh, no … My God, Temple …

STEVE: But who sent that letter? Who is it from, Paul?

TEMPLE: It's signed … ALEX.

FADE IN of closing music.

END OF EPISODE FOUR

EPISODE FIVE

MR WILFRED DAVIS

OPEN TO: *FADE IN STEVE's voice.*

STEVE: But why? What's the point of all this?

TEMPLE: Wait a minute, Steve. I haven't finished reading the letter yet. (*Reading*) "Before leaving the car you will place on the back seat a case containing five thousand pounds. The money must be one pound notes – not numbered consecutively. If the money isn't in the car – or you fail to follow out these instructions – a letter will be forwarded to the press the very next day. This letter will explain in detail the precise reasons for your visit to Cairo in the Spring of 1963.

CARL: (*Softly; frightened*) Oh, no … My God, Temple …

STEVE: But who sent that letter? Who is it from, Paul?

TEMPLE: It's signed … ALEX.

STEVE: ALEX? …

TEMPLE: Yes …

STEVE: Well – suppose ALEX carries out his threat and sends a letter to the press, I fail to see what …

CARL: No, he mustn't! He mustn't do that, Mrs Temple! Whatever happens he mustn't do that!

TEMPLE: (*Quietly*) All right, let's leave that point for the moment. (*A tiny pause*) Before you opened the letter, Lathom, I think you were going to ask me something. I think you were going to ask me whether, in my opinion, the girl in brown has got anything to do with this ALEX affair?

CARL: (*A little surprised*) Yes. Yes, as a matter of fact, I was.

TEMPLE: Well, in my opinion, she does. In fact, so far as the girl in brown is concerned, there seems to me to be one rather significant factor.

CARL: Oh? And what's that?

TEMPLE: You haven't noticed it?

CARL: Why, no! Have you, Mrs Temple?

STEVE: (*Puzzled*) No. I haven't.

TEMPLE: (*With a laugh*) Well, perhaps I'm mistaken. Perhaps it's not so very significant after all. I see this letter was posted in Hampstead … last night …

CARL: Yes.

STEVE: It's been typed on the same machine, darling – the same machine!

CARL: What do you mean, it's been typed on the same machine? Temple, have you ever seen a letter like this before? A letter from … ALEX?

TEMPLE: (*Slowly*) Yes. Mrs Trevelyan received a note from ALEX; it was quite short but …

CARL: (*Staggered*) Mrs Trevelyan? You mean Dr Kohima's secretary?

TEMPLE: Yes.

CARL: And she received a note from … ALEX?

TEMPLE: Yes.

STEVE: Mr Lathom, what are you going to do about this business?

CARL: This business?

TEMPLE: The five thousand pounds?

CARL: Oh, yes! What am I going to do, Temple?

TEMPLE: Well, if you don't want ALEX to write to the newspapers about …

CARL: No! I told you – whatever happens – ALEX musn't be allowed to do that!

TEMPLE: You've only got one alternative.

CARL: What do you mean?

TEMPLE: (*A complete 'let down' for CARL*) You'll have to pay the five thousand pounds.

104

FADE UP of music.

FADE DOWN of music.
A telephone rings and the receiver is lifted.

FORBES: (*Briskly: on the phone*) Hello!

BRADLEY: (*A well-educated young man; on the other end of the line*) Bradley here, sir. We're just about to leave, sir.

FORBES: Good. You understand about the village, Bradley?

BRADLEY: Yes, sir. Perhaps Inspector Crane would like to check the details before we start?

FORBES: I'm afraid Crane isn't here at the moment – I'll check them!

BRADLEY: Very good, sir. (*Briskly, reading*) "Rogers, Thornton, Deal and Makepeace at the village. Carpenter, Hodson, Brown, Briggs and Leaver at the junction near Haybourne ... The cordon consists of Thompson, Bolton, Starting, Hodges, Smith, Hooper, Parker, Hubbard and Snowdon."

FORBES: Right! Now listen, Bradley! Whatever happens once ALEX has reached the car he mustn't get back through the cordon! You understand?

BRADLEY: Yes, sir.

FORBES: Good!

FORBES replaces the receiver.

TEMPLE: Crane's cutting it rather fine, isn't he? It's after nine ...

FORBES: Yes, I know, Temple. I can't understand it. Crane moved out to Golders Green a few days ago and since then he seems ...

The door opens.

FORBES: Oh, here you are, Crane!

CRANE: (*Flustered*) I'm sorry, sir. My car broke down and I had to walk into Hampstead.

FORBES: Bradley was on the phone a few moments ago …

CRANE: Yes, I've had a word with Bradley, sir. We're all set. Oh, you've – er – spoken to Mr Lathom, I presume?

TEMPLE: I had a word with Lathom this morning, Inspector.

CRANE: I expect he's nervous?

TEMPLE: He's nervous; but he'll go through with it all right.

FORBES: I've told Bradley that under no circumstances must ALEX get through the cordon. If he makes a dash for it you've got to stop him.

CRANE: Yes, Sir …

FORBES: Right! (*Turning, ready to leave*) We're meeting Lathom at the garage, I take it?

TEMPLE: Yes. He's waiting for us. Goodbye, Inspector – and good luck.

A moment.

CRANE: Thank you …

FADE UP of music.

CROSS FADE to the sound of a very heavy lift descending to a basement garage.

The lift stops.

The door opens and closes.

TEMPLE: There's Lathom over there.

Footsteps on concrete are heard.

CARL: Oh, hello, Temple! You're rather late.

TEMPLE: Yes, I know. I'm sorry. This is Sir Graham Forbes – Carl Lathom.

CARL: How do you do, sir?

FORBES: Good evening, Mr Lathom. I think Mr Temple has explained to you …

CARL: I know exactly what to do, Sir Graham.

FORBES: When you reach the lane – what's it called, Fallow End? – stop the car, park it in the lane, put the case on the back seat, and walk back to the village. A colleague of mine – Inspector Crane – will be waiting for you at the inn.

CARL: Thank you.

TEMPLE opens the car door.

TEMPLE: Oh! I'm glad to see you've put us a couple of cushions on the floor, Lathom.

CARL: (*A little laugh*) Well – I'd like you both to be as comfortable as possible.

FORBES: We don't have to travel all the way down to Haybourne on the floor, surely, Temple?

TEMPLE: Yes, I think we should, Sir Graham – the car may be tailed from the moment it leaves the garage. We can't take any chances.

CARL: I think he's right, sir.

FORBES: Yes. Yes, perhaps so.

TEMPLE: Now remember what I told you, Lathom. Don't look back – don't talk to us – and above all completely ignore us when you put the attaché case on the seat.

The car door opens.

CARL: (*Nervously but determined*) Yes … yes … don't worry. I'll go through with it all right.

FORBES: I'm sure you will, Mr Lathom. Ready, Temple?

TEMPLE: Yes, I'm ready, Sir Graham.

FORBES: Then let's be off.

The car starts up; it revs up as it moves.

FADE UP of music.

FADE DOWN of music.

FADE UP of a car travelling along a country road.

This is held for a little time and then gradually the car slows down.

The car stops; the engine is switched off.

The car door opens.

CARL LATHOM gets out of the car.

He opens the second door and puts the attaché case on the back seat and closes the door.

He walks away from the car.

A pause.

There is a faint background of wind in the trees and birds singing.

Another pause.

FORBES: (*Very quietly*) I thought he was going to say something when he put the case down.

TEMPLE: (*Also quietly*) Yes …

FORBES: What time do you make it?

TEMPLE: It's nearly half past ten …

FORBES: I could do with a cigarette …

TEMPLE: We daren't risk it …

FORBES: No of course not. (*After a moment*) Listen!

TEMPLE: It's a car …

FORBES: Yes …

TEMPLE: It's coming from the village …

FORBES: (*Softly*) Yes …

FADE UP from the background of a car.

The car draws nearer, passes, and fades away.

A pause.

TEMPLE: I don't think it's stopped …

FORBES: No … (*Quickly*) Wait a minute!

A moment.

In the background, faintly a whistle – rather like a thrush – can be heard.

It stops, and is repeated again.

FORBES: Do you hear that?

TEMPLE: Yes.

FORBES: That's one of Bradley's men …

TEMPLE: He must have seen something …

FORBES: M'm … He must have done …

Pause.

TEMPLE: I think there's someone coming …

FORBES: Listen …

The whistle can be heard again.

A moment.

FORBES: Yes …

TEMPLE: Keep down …

FORBES: Have you got your gun ready …

TEMPLE: Sh!

The visitor can be heard slowly approaching the car; the faint rustle of leaves; the breaking of a twig underfoot.

FORBES: (*Tensely; almost inaudible*) Here … he … is …

TEMPLE: Keep down …

The car door is thrown open, and at precisely that moment the surrounding district springs to life.

Voices, police whistles, etc.

FORBES: Don't move! Don't move, or I'll shoot!

TREVELYAN: (*Terrified*) No! Don't shoot! Don't shoot!!!

FORBES: Why!!!!

TEMPLE: (*Quite pleasantly*) Good evening, Mrs Trevelyan …

FADE UP of music.

Slow FADE DOWN of music.

FADE UP of MRS TREVELYAN who is in a highly emotional and nervous state; sobbing, and dangerously near hysteria.

TREVELYAN: Leave me alone! Please – leave me alone!!!!

TEMPLE: Mrs Trevelyan, don't you realise that we want to help you? Don't you realise we haven't brought you here, to Scotland Yard, just because …

TREVELYAN: Leave me alone! Please! Leave me alone! I've told you all I know …

TEMPLE: You've told us precisely nothing, Mrs Trevelyan. Now listen to what I'm …

FORBES: (*With authority*) Mrs Trevelyan, are you – or are you not – ALEX?

TREVELYAN: Yes! Yes!!! I'm ALEX! I'm ALEX!! (*Sobbing*) Now leave me alone …

FORBES: (*Briskly*) That's all we want to know, Temple! I'll contact the Home Secretary immediately!

TEMPLE: Wait a minute, Sir Graham! (*A moment; seriously*) If you're ALEX, Mrs Trevelyan, there's something I'd like you to explain. Why did you come to my flat that night and confess about the house in Marshall House Terrace? Why did you tell me about the Waverley Hotel at Canterbury?

TREVELYAN: Please! Don't ask me any more questions … (*She starts to cry again*)

TEMPLE: (*Gently*) Now listen to what I'm saying … I know you're distressed about this matter – terribly distressed – but you've got to pull yourself together and tell us the truth.

110

	If you don't tell us the truth, then you know what'll happen … (*Intent on impressing her*) You'll be arrested – tried – and found guilty.
TREVELYAN:	(*Bordering on hysteria; but strangely defiant*) You can't frighten me, Mr Temple! I tell you I'm ALEX! I'm ALEX!!

A pause.

FORBES:	We shall require you to make a detailed statement to that effect, Mrs Trevelyan. Will you do so?
TREVELYAN:	(*Weakly*) Yes.
FORBES:	And you will sign the statement?
TREVELYAN:	Yes – I'll sign it.
FORBES:	Thank you.

The door suddenly opens: FORBES is annoyed.

FORBES:	What is it, Sergeant?
SERGEANT:	Dr Kohima to see you, sir …
TREVELYAN:	Dr Kohima! (*Desperately, urgently*) I don't want to see him! Please! Don't let him in here, I …

DR KOHIMA pushes past the SERGEANT and into the office.

KOHIMA:	(*Angrily*) What is the meaning of this? What is my secretary doing here?
SERGEANT:	Just a moment, sir – you can't force your way into …
FORBES:	(*Quietly*) That's all right, Sergeant!
SERGEANT:	Very good, sir.

The door closes.

FORBES:	Now, Dr Kohima, what's the trouble?
KOHIMA:	You might well ask, sir! Why is my secretary detained here at Scotland Yard?

TEMPLE:	How did you know that you'd find Mrs Trevelyan here at Scotland Yard?
KOHIMA:	This morning, Mr Temple, if you don't mind, I will ask the questions!
TREVELYAN:	Dr Kohima, please don't interfere! I beg of you …
KOHIMA:	You look ill, my dear! What has happened to you?
TEMPLE:	It's not surprising that Mrs Trevelyan looks ill! Apart from spending last night in gaol she insists …
KOHIMA:	In gaol! Are you joking?
FORBES:	No, we're not joking, Dr Kohima.
KOHIMA:	But – but what does this mean?
FORBES:	It means that Mrs Trevelyan … is … ALEX.
KOHIMA:	(*Astonished*) What!!!! You can't be serious, why … Mr Temple, do you think that Mrs Trevelyan is ALEX?
TEMPLE:	Mrs Trevelyan says that she is quite willing to make a statement to that effect, and that she is quite willing to sign such a statement.
KOHIMA:	Mrs Trevelyan isn't in a fit state to sign any statement – not at the moment.
FORBES:	What do you mean?
KOHIMA:	(*Almost rasping out his words*) I mean, my dear Sir Graham, that Mrs Trevelyan is tired – emotionally unbalanced; under such circumstances it would be grossly unfair to ask her to …
FORBES:	Even if Mrs Trevelyan doesn't make that statement …

TREVELYAN: (*Still distressed*) Oh, Doctor, please – leave me alone and don't interfere.

KOHIMA: (*Firmly*) Sir Graham, Mrs Trevelyan is not only my secretary, she is a patient of mine, and therefore I positively insist that she is permitted to rest for at least two hours ...

FORBES: (*A moment*) Very well ...

TREVELYAN: I couldn't rest! Not now! Oh, do leave me alone! Please, I implore you ... do leave me alone!

KOHIMA: (*With a strange authority*) Come over here, Barbara.

A moment.

KOHIMA: Sit down, my dear.

TREVELYAN: Why did you come here?

KOHIMA: (*Quietly*) Look at me. Don't be afraid ... Look at me, Barbara ...

A pause.

Dead silence.

KOHIMA: You are tired?

TREVELYAN: (*Tensely*) Yes, terribly tired ...

KOHIMA: Don't turn your head away ... Look at me ...

TREVELYAN: (*A moment*) No ...questions, Charles?

KOHIMA: No questions, my dear.

TREVELYAN: (*A note of relief*) It – it – it was good of you to come, I didn't really expect that you would.

KOHIMA: Don't talk ... Don't excite yourself ... (*A tiny pause*) Don't talk, Barbara ... You are still ... tired ...?

TREVELYAN: Yes.

KOHIMA: (*Slowly*) But everything is going to be all right now, you know that ...

113

TREVELYAN: (*Mechanically; almost as if talking in her sleep*) Yes, Charles, everything is going to be all right …

KOHIMA: (*Slowly; soothingly*) There is no need to worry, Barbara …

TREVELYAN: There … is … no … need … to … worry …

KOHIMA: (*Very softly*) That's right. (*A moment*) Put your head down on the cushion … Gently … (*After a pause*) You can close your eyes now …

A very long pause.

FORBES: Temple, she's asleep!

TEMPLE: Yes …

KOHIMA: So! … (*A slight pause; then in a normal voice*) Why are you smiling, my friend?

TEMPLE: I was just thinking, doctor. You can lead a horse to water but you can't make him drink.

KOHIMA: Now what do you mean by that, Mr Temple?

TEMPLE: (*Significantly*) I think you know what I mean, Dr Kohima …

FADE UP of music.

FADE DOWN of music.

A key in a lock can be heard followed by the opening of a door.

STEVE: Hello, darling!

The door closes.

TEMPLE: Oh, hello, Steve! I'm sorry I'm late, I've only just left the Yard. Where's Ricky?

114

STEVE: He's gone to the pictures. I'll take your coat. (*A moment*) There's someone to see you, it's that Welshman we met at …

TEMPLE: Davis? What does he want?

STEVE: I don't know, darling – he's in the drawing room. (*Quietly*) I suppose you've seen the newspapers?

TEMPLE: Yes.

STEVE: They're making an awful fuss about Mrs Trevelyan. The Evening Graphic says …

TEMPLE: If it hadn't been for Crane the newspapers wouldn't have got hold of the story! The fool opened his mouth a yard wide the moment he got back to town. Anyhow, let's see what our Welsh friend has got to say. How long has he been here?

STEVE: Only about two or three minutes.

TEMPLE: Oh.

The lounge door opens.

TEMPLE: Hello, Davis – what can I do for you?

The door closes.

DAVIS: (*Pleasantly, but with his faintly bewildered air*) Well, I don't know that you can do anything, Mr Temple. I suppose really it's sheer impertinence on my part to trouble you like this, but – well – the fact of the matter is, Mr Temple, something rather peculiar happened last night … the night I stayed in Canterbury, at the Waverley.

TEMPLE: Oh?

DAVIS: Most peculiar … I don't like to make a mountain out of a mole hill, as the saying goes, but …

TEMPLE: What happened … exactly …?

115

DAVIS: Well, you remember, after I left your table I went upstairs to my room. My room, by the way, was number 26. Actually, that was next to the room that you and Mrs Temple intended to occupy. Well, when I turned into the corridor I saw someone go into your room. A most nervous, suspicious looking individual …

TEMPLE: Go on …

DAVIS: This made me rather curious – so curious in fact that I tiptoed up to the door and peeped through the keyhole. I suppose it was rather wicked of me, but …

STEVE: What did you see, Mr Davis?

DAVIS: I saw this fellow, Mrs Temple – open your suitcase and take out a silver flask. He did something to the flask. I don't know what it was because at that moment he turned his back on me, but I'm sure that …

TEMPLE: What was he like, Davis – this suspicious looking character?

DAVIS: Well, to be truthful, I think it was Mr Chester, sir. The man who runs the hotel. Mr Frank Chester.

FADE IN closing music.

END OF EPISODE FIVE

EPISODE SIX

MR LEO BRENT

OPEN TO: *FADE IN STEVE's voice.*

STEVE: What did you see, Mr Davis?

DAVIS: I saw this fellow, Mrs Temple – open your suitcase and take out a silver flask. He did something to the flask. I don't know what it was because at that moment he turned his back on me, but I'm sure that …

TEMPLE: What was he like, Davis – this suspicious looking character?

DAVIS: Well, to be truthful, I think it was Mr Chester, sir. The man who runs the hotel. Mr Frank Chester. I think you know who I mean?

TEMPLE: Yes, I know who you mean. Is that all you wanted to tell me?

DAVIS: Lordy, no! I haven't got to the real point. Not by a long chalk. (*Unable to conceal his excitement*) Late that night, after you and Mrs Temple had departed, I went downstairs to have a glass of ale. I put my hand in my pocket to pay for the drink and – to my complete astonishment I found this note. Let me read it to you! Let me tell you what it says! (*A moment; reading*) "No matter what happens Mrs Trevelyan isn't ALEX. MRS TREVELYAN ISN'T ALEX. ALEX – is – the – girl – in – brown".

STEVE: The girl in brown!

DAVIS: Yes! (*Completely baffled*) Now I ask you! What on earth does that mean?

There is a moment's pause, then TEMPLE commences to laugh. He is obviously highly amused.

STEVE: Paul!!!!

TEMPLE is still laughing …

119

DAVIS: (B*ewildered*) Have I said something very funny or something …?

TEMPLE: No! Please forgive me, Mr Davis, I'm terribly sorry.

STEVE: Do you mind if I have a look at that note, Mr Davis?

DAVIS: No, of course not …

A moment.

STEVE: It's not typed, Paul …

TEMPLE: So I see.

DAVIS: I was wondering if we could have the handwriting tested at all – isn't there some sort of system – rather like the fingerprint system?

TEMPLE: As a means of comparison, yes, Mr Davis. But if you want my personal opinion …

DAVIS: You don't think this note was actually written by ALEX?

TEMPLE: Since you ask me – I don't.

DAVIS: Why don't you think so?

TEMPLE: Well, in the first place, the other notes have been type-written, and secondly …

DAVIS: Yes …?

TEMPLE: And secondly … (*He hesitates, then quickly off-hand*) I just don't think it was written by ALEX.

DAVIS: Well, I'm sure it's all very confusing.

STEVE: But if the note wasn't written by ALEX, darling, then how did it come to be in Mr Davis's pocket?

DAVIS: That's what I'd like to know!

TEMPLE: It was obviously put there, Mr Davis, by the person who wrote it, but in my humble opinion the person who wrote it wasn't ALEX.

DAVIS: (*More bewildered than ever*) I see. (*A moment; reflectively*) At least, I – think I see.

TEMPLE and STEVE laugh, and then DAVIS laughs too.

DAVIS: Well, I'm sorry to have made a nuisance of myself.

TEMPLE: On the contrary, you've been most helpful.

DAVIS: (*Pleased with himself*) Thank you, Mr Temple. As a matter of fact I'm going down to Canterbury again shortly. I suppose now you wouldn't like me to …

There is a knock and the door opens.

STEVE: Why – I thought you were out, Ricky!

RICKY: Only for a little while, madam. So sorry if you were inconvenienced …

STEVE: Oh, no – that's all right …

DAVIS: Well – I'll be off!

RICKY: (*Pleasantly surprised*) Good evening, sir.

DAVIS: Er – good evening.

RICKY: Don't you remember me?

DAVIS: I'm – I'm afraid I don't.

RICKY: Ricky!

DAVIS: Er – Ricky?

RICKY: (*Surprised*) Ricky, sir! Hotel Nevada, Twenty-Third Street, New York …

DAVIS: (*Laughing*) I'm – I'm afraid there must be some mistake. I've never been to New York.

RICKY: (*Seriously; surprised*) You don't remember me, Mr Cartwright?

DAVIS: My name is Davis – Wilfred Davis.

RICKY: Davis?

DAVIS: Yes …

A moment.

RICKY: (*Seriously*) Sorry. So sorry.

DAVIS: Oh, that's all right. We all make mistakes.

121

STEVE: Mr Davis is leaving, Ricky.

RICKY: This way, sir.

The door opens.

DAVIS: Well, goodbye. It's been very nice seeing you both again; I only hope I haven't made a nuisance of myself.

TEMPLE: No, of course not!

The door closes.

STEVE: Do you think that Ricky …

TEMPLE: Sh! Wait a minute!

A moment.

The door opens.

RICKY: Would you like me to clean the silver, madam, before I …

TEMPLE: Ricky …

RICKY: Mr Temple?

TEMPLE: Why did you call Mr Davis … Mr Cartwright?

RICKY: Why did you call Mr Cartwright … Mr Davis?

STEVE: We know him as Mr Davis.

RICKY: I know him as Mr Cartwright.

STEVE: But he isn't Mr Cartwright, Ricky – he's Mr Davis.

RICKY: (*A moment*) Then I made a mistake. I'm so sorry.

TEMPLE: No! You didn't make a mistake, Ricky, and you know you didn't! You met Davis in New York at the Nevada Hotel. He called himself Cartwright.

RICKY: Yes …

TEMPLE: When was this?

RICKY: Last year, January – February – March. You see for three months I work in the hotel. Mr Cartwright – he has an apartment on the second floor. (*A moment*) Mr Davis – Mr Cartwright –

122

same face … same person … I don't make mistake.

TEMPLE: No, I don't think you do, Ricky – (*A moment; his thoughts elsewhere*) Thank you …

RICKY: Thank you, Mr Temple.

The door closes.

STEVE: Darling, if Davis isn't all that he pretends to be, then why on earth does …

STEVE is interrupted by the telephone, and TEMPLE immediately answers it.

TEMPLE: (*On the phone*) Hello?

CRANE: (*On the other end of the line*) Is that you, Mr Temple?

TEMPLE: Oh, hello, Inspector.

CRANE: I'm speaking for Sir Graham.

TEMPLE: Yes.

CRANE: Do you think you could manage to get back to the Yard?

TEMPLE: (*Irritatedly*) Tonight?

CRANE: Yes.

TEMPLE: Well …

CRANE: It's rather important.

TEMPLE: (*A moment*) Yes, all right, Crane – tell Sir Graham I'll be there in about half an hour.

CRANE: Very good.

TEMPLE replaces the receiver.

TEMPLE: Darling, listen! I've got an appointment at nine-fifteen with an old friend of mine called Brent – Leo Brent. I'm supposed to be meeting him at Luigi's in the Haymarket. I want you to go along there and keep him company – don't let him go, Steve, I particularly want to see him.

STEVE: Leo Brent?

TEMPLE: You remember him, Steve! You met him several years ago at Juan. He's an American. Tall, fair, rather good looking.

STEVE: (*Pleasantly impressed by the memory of LEO BRENT*) Oh, yes … yes, I remember …

TEMPLE: (*Mimicking STEVE*) I thought you would! (*About to depart*) O.K., Steve, I'll see you about …

STEVE: Darling, wait a minute.

A moment.

TEMPLE: Well?

STEVE: You told Davis that you didn't believe that note, found in his pocket, was written by ALEX.

TEMPLE: I don't think it <u>was</u> written by ALEX.

STEVE: Then who do you think wrote it?

A pause.

TEMPLE: Since you ask me – I think it was written by … Mr Davis.

STEVE: By Mr Davis …?

TEMPLE: Yes, darling …

STEVE: But why should he do a thing like that?

TEMPLE: Steve, I can't explain now, I've got to …

A moment.

STEVE: Don't you think Davis was telling the truth?

TEMPLE: About the flask?

STEVE: Yes.

TEMPLE: Well – he didn't see Chester take the flask out of the suitcase, I'm pretty sure about that.

STEVE: What makes you so sure?

TEMPLE: He couldn't have seen him – at least – not through the keyhole.

STEVE: How do you know?

TEMPLE:	Don't you remember, darling? The room didn't have a keyhole, at least, not one you could see through – it had a Yale lock.
STEVE:	A Yale ... Oh, yes. Yes, I ought to have thought of that.
TEMPLE:	(*Faintly amused*) Yes, darling – you ought to have thought of it. I'll see you at Luigi's!
STEVE:	Don't be too late!
TEMPLE:	(*At the door*) And be nice to Brent!

The door opens.

STEVE:	I certainly will.
TEMPLE:	But, not too nice!

STEVE laughs.

FADE UP of music.

FADE DOWN of music.

FADE UP of SIR GRAHAM FORBES; he is extremely annoyed and on the verge of losing his temper.

FORBES:	I take it that you now refuse to make a statement ...
TREVELYAN:	(*Calmly*) I refuse to make any statement whatsoever, Sir Graham. Surely I've made that perfectly clear?
FORBES:	Two hours ago, Mrs Trevelyan, you gave me to understand that ...
KOHIMA:	Two hours ago, Sir Graham, Mrs Trevelyan was in an extremely emotional, one might almost say, a completely unbalanced state of mind. I told you so at the time.
FORBES:	You told us a great many things at the time, Dr Kohima – I'm fully aware of that. But the point is this! Mrs Trevelyan said that she was ALEX, therefore ...

KOHIMA: (*Slowly, but with confidence*) You know perfectly well that Mrs Trevelyan isn't ALEX. If you thought for one moment that Mrs Trevelyan was ALEX you wouldn't be wasting your time like this.

FORBES: Why did you go to Haybourne last night, Mrs Trevelyan? (*A moment*) How did you know about Carl Lathom and the five thousand pounds?

KOHIMA: Don't answer him, Barbara!

FORBES: (*Raising his voice*) You heard what I said! Why did you go to Haybourne last night?

KOHIMA: (*After a moment; slowly*) There's only one answer to that question, my friend. Mrs Trevelyan went to Haybourne because ... (*A moment's hesitation*) she was sent there.

TREVELYAN: (*Tensely*) Charles, please!

FORBES: I beg to differ, Dr Kohima. There are two possible answers to my question. Either Mrs Trevelyan went to Haybourne because, as you say, she was sent there, or because she instructed Lathom to deliver the five thousand pounds!

KOHIMA: (*With almost a powerful sincerity*) Sir Graham, I give you my word – I give you my personal assurance – that Mrs Trevelyan is not ALEX!

The office door opens.

A moment.

FORBES: What is it, Inspector?

CRANE: Mr Temple's arrived – he's in my office.

FORBES: Thank you, Crane. (*After a moment's hesitation*) I ... shall ... be back in a moment, Mrs Trevelyan.

FORBES goes out of the office door, closing the door behind him.

He enters the second office.

FORBES: I'm sorry to drag you back to the Yard, Temple.

TEMPLE: That's all right, Sir Graham. What's happened?

FORBES: I think you know what's happened, Temple.

CRANE: She won't talk.

TEMPLE: So Mrs Trevelyan's changed her mind?

FORBES: Yes.

TEMPLE: Well – that doesn't make any difference. You've still got proof that she turned up at Haybourne last night.

FORBES: (*Worried*) That isn't the point, Temple …

TEMPLE: There's a doubt in your mind?

FORBES: Quite frankly – yes. Last night I felt pretty sure, as you know, that Mrs Trevelyan was ALEX; but somehow, when she turned up at Haybourne …

TEMPLE: You thought it was just a little bit too obvious?

FORBES: Yes. You see, Temple – we know that ALEX is a blackmailer – a blackmailer on quite, well, quite an unprecedented scale. We know for instance that he blackmailed Norma Rice, Richard East, Carl Lathom, and even Sir Ernest Cranbury …

CRANE: We're now pretty certain, sir, that for every case we've heard of there must be other poor devils suffering in silence.

FORBES: But the point is this, Temple. Did he blackmail Mrs Trevelyan into turning up at Haybourne and into confessing that she was ALEX?

TEMPLE: Yes, I think he did.

FORBES: Then you don't think Mrs Trevelyan is ALEX?

127

TEMPLE: No, I don't think she is ALEX.

CRANE: And neither do I! In fact, if you want my opinion I think ALEX is Dr Kohima.

TEMPLE: And what makes you think that?

CRANE: Well, to begin with – the car incident. It was his car that smashed into you and Mrs Temple the night Sir Ernest was murdered. Secondly, don't forget that we found his pencil by the body of James Barton.

TEMPLE: But he claims that it wasn't his pencil, Inspector.

CRANE: Now I ask you! Do you think that pencil belongs to Dr Kohima – or don't you?

TEMPLE: (*Smiling*) I think it does, Inspector.

FORBES: And yet you don't believe that Dr Kohima is ALEX?

TEMPLE: I didn't say that, Sir Graham. (*A laugh*) By Timothy, I didn't say that!

FORBES: (*Rather puzzled*) Temple, I've been meaning to ask you. The night that Barton was murdered you were staying in Canterbury – at the Waverley.

TEMPLE: Yes.

CRANE: What made you go down to Canterbury?

TEMPLE: (*Glibly*) I told you what happened at Canterbury, Inspector. I told you about Frank Chester, or rather Mulberry, about Wilfred Davis bumping into us and …

CRANE: (*Faintly irritated*) We know what happened at Canterbury, sir, but the point is, why did you go down to Canterbury in the first place?

TEMPLE: I – er – I went down to see an old friend of mine.

CRANE: M'm. I see.

128

FORBES: (*Worried*) I don't know what to do about Mrs
            Trevelyan, Temple. If we don't arrest …
TEMPLE: Well, whatever you do, Sir Graham – keep an
            eye on her.
CRANE: You think she's in danger, Temple?
TEMPLE: Yes, Inspector, I think she's in danger. (*A
            moment, then suddenly*) Well, I must be off!
            I'm supposed to be at Luigi's by now.
CRANE: (*A little surprised*) Luigi's? In the Haymarket?
TEMPLE: Yes.
CRANE: (*Pleasantly*) I'm meeting a friend there later in
            the evening, Temple – we might get together.
TEMPLE: Yes, why not? (*A moment*) I'll buy you a drink,
            Inspector.
CRANE: (*Laughing*) Thanks very much.
TEMPLE: Goodnight, Sir Graham.
FORBES: (*Still worried*) Goodbye, Temple …
FADE UP of music.

FADE DOWN of music.
*FADE UP of a small dance orchestra; rather a
sophisticated, yet sentimental number.*
The number finishes; it is followed by slight applause.
*FADE UP of LEO BRENT. He is an American; about forty-
five and very likeable.*
BRENT: … So I took one look at the guy, and I said
            "Waiter, is this supposed to be fresh fruit?"
            And he said, "Sure it's fresh – I've just opened
            the can …"
STEVE: (*Laughing*) I don't believe one word of it, Mr
            Brent.
BRENT: Mrs Temple, so long as I live and breathe I
            swear …   Well, it's a good story anyway.

129

	(*Suddenly*) Is that the time? I ought to be making a move …
STEVE:	I'm sure Paul will be here any minute now, Mr Brent …
BRENT:	(*Raising his voice*) Say, Flora, is there a telephone around here?
FLORA:	The line's out of order, sir – but there's a box downstairs in the vestibule.
BRENT:	Thanks. Will you excuse me, Mrs Temple, I'd like to phone? I had another date at ten o'clock and – well – redheads get impatient.
STEVE:	(*Laughing*) Go right ahead.
BRENT:	Thanks. I shan't be long.

The dance orchestra starts again.

FLORA:	Can I get you another drink, madam?
STEVE:	No, I don't think so, thanks.
CARL:	Certainly you can, Flora – make it two dry martinis.
STEVE:	Why, hello, Mr Lathom!
CARL:	(*Laughing*) Hello, Mrs Temple! And what are you doing here?
STEVE:	Well, if you must know I'm waiting for my husband.
CARL:	I say, that's a new slant on things. Man bites dog – wife waits for husband.

CARL and STEVE laugh.

FLORA:	Two dry martinis, sir.
CARL:	Thank you, Flora. (*Takes drink*) Skol!
STEVE:	Skol!

A moment.

CARL:	I suppose you – heard what happened last night?
STEVE:	Mrs Trevelyan?

CARL: Yes. Extraordinary business! I really can't
           believe it! I really can't believe it! Do you
           know, when I woke up this morning and
           realised what had happened last night I …
STEVE: You thought you'd dreamt it …
CARL: I did! Honestly, I did! I mean … Mrs Trevelyan
           … she's such a nice sort of person.
STEVE: I'm afraid it's always the nice sort of people
           that … Oh, hello, darling!
TEMPLE: (*A little out of breath*) Hello, Steve! Where's
           Leo?
STEVE: He's downstairs – phoning.
TEMPLE: Oh, good – I was afraid he'd gone. (*Pleasantly*)
           Well – how's Mr Lathom this evening?
CARL: Well, I'm feeling a little better this evening
           than I did this morning. I was telling Mrs
           Temple, even now I really can't believe it!
TEMPLE: You can't believe what?
CARL: That Mrs Trevelyan is ALEX. Oh, I know she
           turned up at Haybourne last night, and
           according to the newspapers she's already
           confessed, but … but … even so I really can't
           believe it. I mean … Mrs Trevelyan … of all
           people!
LEO BRENT returns.
BRENT: So you finally made it!
TEMPLE: (*Laughing*) Oh, hello, Leo! I'm sorry I'm late.
BRENT: That's o.k., you got here!
TEMPLE and BRENT laugh.
STEVE: Oh, Mr Lathom, this is a friend of my
           husband's – Leo Brent
CARL: How do you do?
BRENT: Glad to know you.
A slightly awkward pause.

131

STEVE:	Well …
BRENT:	What are you drinking, Mr Lathom?
CARL:	If you don't mind I think I'll be making a move. Goodnight, Mrs Temple.
STEVE:	Goodnight, Mr Latham.
TEMPLE:	Goodnight.
BRENT:	Goodnight.

A moment.

TEMPLE:	So you got my message all right, Leo?
BRENT:	Sure I got it! Meet me at Luigi's, you said – at nine-fifteen. At – er – nine-fifteen.
TEMPLE:	Yes, I'm sorry about that, but I got all tied up and …
BRENT:	You're telling me!
TEMPLE:	Let's go over in the corner where we can talk. (*Calling*) Flora, two more martinis – and – what are you drinking, Leo?
BRENT:	I'll have a Bronx.
TEMPLE:	And a Bronx, please.
FLORA:	Yes, sir.

FADE UP slightly of orchestra and background noises.

The orchestra stops; FADE background noises almost completely.
FADE UP of TEMPLE.

TEMPLE:	Well, there you are, Leo – that's the proposition.
BRENT:	How long would you want me to stay in Canterbury?
TEMPLE:	That depends. I'd certainly like you to stay down there for three or four days.
BRENT:	M'm – I take it that you don't think this guy himself – Chester – or Mulberry if you like – is really ALEX?

TEMPLE: No, I'm certain he isn't. But I'm equally certain that Chester's in frequent contact with ALEX. That's why I want you to go down to Canterbury, Leo. You're not known down there, you don't look particularly …

BRENT: Intelligent …

TEMPLE and BRENT laugh.

TEMPLE: Well, you said it!

BRENT: Yeah, it sounds a pretty good set up. I get the angle. American tourist complete with camera, shooting-stick and …

STEVE: Acute dyspepsia! But don't overdo it!

BRENT: You leave that to me, Mrs Temple. There's just one point, Temple.

TEMPLE: Yes?

BRENT: Well, supposing Chester catches on and things get pretty hectic?

TEMPLE: You can handle that situation, Leo!

BRENT: Oh, sure! I'm not worried about that, but – well – supposing I find out something – something pretty big.

TEMPLE: Phone me. Phone me every morning between seven and ten and every night between ten and midnight. If I don't get a call from you I'll be down in two hours.

BRENT: O.K., leave it to me.

TEMPLE: Thanks, Leo. Thanks a lot.

BRENT: That's all right. Oh, there's just one point. If, by any chance, you don't hear from me, and when you get down to Canterbury I don't appear to be kicking around, well … (*With a little laugh*) Don't forget – it's all done by mirrors.

TEMPLE: (*Suddenly remembering*) Oh, yes! Yes, I shan't forget.

BRENT: O.K.! Goodnight, Mrs Temple – next time we meet I'll make it Steve.

STEVE: Goodbye, Leo!

A pause.

LEO BRENT departs.

STEVE: He's an awfully nice fellow!

TEMPLE: Yes, one of the best. We used to share a room together, you know – way back when we were in New York. (*Laughing*) We had rather an inquisitive landlady – that's what he meant when he said it's all done by mirrors. If either of us had a message he wanted to leave we used to write it down and stick it behind the mirror on the dressing table – usually with chewing gum.

STEVE: How old would he be?

TEMPLE: Leo? Oh, he must be about … Oh, somewhere in his middle forties now … Hello! Here's our friend Lathom again!

CARL: I say, Temple – I'm sorry to chip in like this, but your man's downstairs and he seems to be in rather a flap.

STEVE: Ricky, do you mean?

CARL: Yes.

TEMPLE: Downstairs?

CARL: Yes, he's in the vestibule. Apparently he tried to get through on the telephone but the line's out of order.

STEVE: (*Anxiously*) Has something happened …?

CARL: Well, to be quite frank, I can't understand what he's talking about. He said that shortly after you left the flat a girl turned up and said she

134

	particularly wanted to see you. Ricky seems to think it's frightfully important.
STEVE:	A girl? What sort of a girl?
CARL:	I don't know. I'm not even sure that he knows himself. I think perhaps you'd … (*A sudden hesitation*) I say, Temple, I – suppose it couldn't possibly be that girl – the one that followed Mrs Temple – the girl in brown …
TEMPLE:	Where is Ricky – near the cloakroom?
CARL:	Yes … just over on the other side.
TEMPLE:	O.K. Thanks. Come along, Steve!

FADE UP of background noises and orchestra.
FADE UP to a peak then gradually FADE completely down.
FADE SCENE.

FADE UP of vestibule noises; in the background the cloakroom attendant can be heard.

CLOAKROOM ATTENDANT:	Number 24 … is it a dark coat, sir? … Thank you, sir. Don't forget to ask for the valise sir …
TEMPLE:	Hello, Ricky! What's all the excitement about?
RICKY:	(*Rather perturbed*) So sorry to have interrupted you, sir – but after Mrs Temple left a young lady called at the flat. She said it was most important – most important that she speak to you. I tried to telephone you, sir, but I could not get through …
TEMPLE:	That's all right, Ricky …
STEVE:	Is she still at the house?
RICKY:	Yes …
TEMPLE:	What's she like … this girl … this young lady?
RICKY:	Oh, very nice. Very pretty – but most worried.
TEMPLE:	(*A shade impatient*) Yes, I know – but what does she look like?

135

RICKY: She's dressed in brown, sir. Brown shoes, brown handbag, brown …

TEMPLE: Right, Ricky!

STEVE: Where's the car?

TEMPLE: It's in the mews on the corner – I'll start it while you get your coat.

STEVE: Yes, all right, dear.

TEMPLE: Come along, Ricky!!!

FADE UP of music.

FADE DOWN of music.

FADE UP of a car ticking over.

RICKY: Here's Mrs Temple, sir!

TEMPLE: Oh, good!

The car door opens and closes.

STEVE: Sorry to keep you darling! I couldn't find the ticket for my coat.

TEMPLE: That's all right.

The car revs up and drives away – followed almost immediately by the loud explosion of a burst tyre.

STEVE: (*Quietly; tensely*) What's that!

TEMPLE: Need you ask? What is it?! Oh, Lord …

The car slows down then stops.

TEMPLE gets out.

A moment.

STEVE: (*Raising her voice*) Which tyre is it?

TEMPLE: The front – left hand side.

RICKY: There's glass right across the road, sir.

TEMPLE: Yes – right across the road, Ricky. It's a broken bottle …

TEMPLE kicks the glass.

TEMPLE: … by the look of things.

STEVE: That's rather odd, isn't it, darling …? Glass –
            stretching right across the entrance to the mews
            …

TEMPLE: Yes …

STEVE: It looks as if it's been put there deliberately.

TEMPLE: So that we'd waste time changing the wheel!
            But that's precisely what we're not going to do!
            (*Quickly*) Jump out, Steve! Ricky, get on the
            other side of the …

As TEMPLE speaks a taxi suddenly draws level with them.

TEMPLE: Hello … Who's this?

KOHIMA: (*Calling from the taxi*) Mr Temple, are you in
            trouble?

TEMPLE: Oh, hello, Dr Kohima!

TEMPLE crosses to the taxi.

KOHIMA: (*Seriously*) I wanted to have a chat with you,
            Mr Temple, and Sir Graham Forbes said that
            you were at Luigi's so I decided to …

TEMPLE: Is this your taxi?

KOHIMA: Why … yes …

TEMPLE: Jump in, Steve! (*Calling*) Clear the glass away,
            Ricky! Quick!!!

TEMPLE opens the taxi door.

DRIVER: (*Through the partition window*) 'Ere, what's
            the game, mate?

KOHIMA: (*Sensing the urgency*) That's all right, driver!
            Where do you wish to go to, Mr Temple?

TEMPLE: Eaton Square!

The door closes.

TEMPLE: And step on it!!!

DRIVER: (*Resigned*) Okey-doke …

The taxi revs up.

TEMPLE: (*He lowers the window and shouts*) We'll see
            you back at the house, Ricky!!!!

KOHIMA: I … don't think we've met, Mrs Temple, but …
TEMPLE: Oh, sorry … Dr Kohima … my wife …
KOHIMA: Sit here, Mrs Temple, I …
TEMPLE: (*Interrupting KOHIMA*) Step on it, driver!!!!
FADE UP of music.

FADE DOWN of music.
The taxi is drawing into the kerb.
The taxi door opens.
TEMPLE: Do you mind waiting in the taxi for a few minutes, Doctor – I shan't keep you long?
KOHIMA: (*A little surprised*) No. No, that's all right …
TEMPLE: Here's ten shillings – thank you very much.
DRIVER: Oh! Thank you, sir!
TEMPLE: Have you got your key, darling?
STEVE: Yes, I think it's in my handbag.
FADE scene.

FADE UP of STEVE producing her key.
TEMPLE: (*Quickly*) The door's open …
STEVE: Yes … so it is …
TEMPLE: Quiet, darling …
STEVE: Why …
TEMPLE: Sh!
The front door opens quietly.
TEMPLE: She'll be in the drawing room.
A second door opens.
STEVE: No, darling, there's no one in … (*She gives a sudden cry of horror*) She's on the floor! Paul, she's been shot …
TEMPLE: Take it easy, darling!
STEVE: Oh it's horrible!
TEMPLE: Steady, darling …
A moment.

138

STEVE: (*A tiny pause*) Is she …?

TEMPLE: (*After a moment*) Yes, she's dead. (*Tensely*) This must have happened about … (*He stops dead; listening*)

STEVE: What is it? (*Another pause*) What is it, Paul?

TEMPLE: Listen!!!

From the cloakroom the sound of water can be heard running into the wash hand basin.

STEVE: There's somebody in the cloakroom!

TEMPLE: Yes … Darling, get me that gun – top drawer of the desk!

A drawer opens and closes.

STEVE: Here it is …

TEMPLE: Thanks …

STEVE: Why are you putting it in your pocket, so that no one can see it?

TEMPLE: Sh! Stand over there, Steve – near the door! (*Raising his voice*) Do you mind coming out of the cloakroom?!!!!

A moment.

The water in the cloakroom is turned off.

Another pause.

TEMPLE: (*With force and authority*) I said: DO YOU MIND COMING OUT OF THE CLOAKROOM?!!!

The cloakroom door opens.

CRANE: Not at all, Mr Temple!

STEVE: (*Aghast*) Inspector Crane!!!!

FADE UP of closing music.

END OF EPISODE SIX

EPISODE SEVEN

THE GIRL IN BROWN

OPEN TO: *FADE UP the sound of running water.*
The sound of water running into the wash hand basin can be heard coming from the cloakroom.

STEVE: There's – There's somebody in the cloakroom!

TEMPLE: Yes … (*A quick, tense whisper*) Darling, get me that gun – it's in the top drawer of the desk!

A drawer opens and closes.

STEVE: Here you are.

TEMPLE: Thanks …

STEVE: Why are you putting it in your pocket, so that no one can see it?

TEMPLE: Sh! Stand over there, Steve – near the door! (*Raising his voice*) Do you mind coming out of the cloakroom?!!!!

A moment.

The water in the cloakroom is turned off.

Another pause.

TEMPLE: (*With force and authority*) I said: DO YOU MIND COMING OUT OF THE CLOAKROOM?!!!

The cloakroom door opens.

CRANE: Not at all, Mr Temple!

STEVE: Inspector Crane!!!!

CRANE: So you've finally arrived, Temple.

TEMPLE: Yes. (*After a moment's pause; quite casually*) I see you've cut your hand, Inspector. What did you cut it on – a piece of glass?

CRANE: (*Rather surprised*) Why, yes! I've just been cleaning it up. I'm afraid I've been using your cloakroom … I hope you don't mind?

TEMPLE: No, of course not. What happened?

CRANE: You might well ask, sir! I went to Luigi's, but apparently I just missed you. I wanted to have a chat with you, Temple, so I came on here. I really can't understand why you didn't get here first.

TEMPLE: Can't you, Inspector? However, go on …

CRANE: Well, there's not a lot more to tell. I was coming up …

STEVE gives a slight moan, as if she is about to faint.

CRANE: Why, Mrs Temple!

TEMPLE: Steve!

STEVE: It's all right, darling, I just feel rather faint, that's all. It was such a shock just now … I think I'll go and lie down for a little while.

CRANE: By all means.

TEMPLE: Yes, I should, darling.

A door opens and closes.

A moment.

CRANE: Well, as I was saying, I was coming up to the house when I heard a shot. I dashed in and – well – this girl was more or less … as she is now.

TEMPLE: Was the house empty?

CRANE: Yes, but I found one of the bedroom windows open, one of the windows leading on to the fire escape.

TEMPLE: But how did you cut your hand, exactly?

CRANE: Oh yes. I'm sorry about that, but I'm afraid in my excitement I knocked the glass off your wife's dressing table.

TEMPLE: I see.

CRANE: I suppose you recognise this girl?

TEMPLE: It's the girl I told you about. The one who followed my wife from Marshall House Terrace. The girl in brown …

CRANE: Yes. Did you know that this girl was here … waiting for you?

TEMPLE: Of course! That's why I left Luigi's. Ricky turned up there and told me that she particularly wanted to see me. I made up my … (*Suddenly; a complete change*) Look here, Inspector, I've got Dr Kohima waiting for me downstairs so …

CRANE: Dr Kohima!

TEMPLE: Yes, he gave me a lift home in a taxi. I had some trouble with my car. If you'll excuse me?

CRANE: Yes, of course.

The door opens.

TEMPLE: Hello, Ricky!

RICKY: (*Nervously*) Mrs Temple has just told me about the young lady, sir. It is most distressing.

CRANE: Oh, you're Ricky are you? Yes, of course! Come here, young man, I'd rather like to have a word with you.

TEMPLE: This is Inspector Crane, Ricky.

CRANE: Now it appears, from what I can gather, that you were the last person to see this young lady alive, Ricky.

RICKY: Correction, please!

CRANE: (*Taken aback*) What's that?

RICKY: Not the last person, sir.

CRANE: (*Surprised*) No?

RICKY: No.

CRANE: Then who was the last person?

A moment.

RICKY: (*Blandly*) If you please, Mr Crane … the murderer.

FADE UP of music.

FADE DOWN of music.

TEMPLE: I'm sorry to keep you waiting, Dr Kohima!

KOHIMA: That's quite all right, Mr Temple.

TEMPLE: Driver, I want you to take me back to Luigi's and then on to an address in – in South Kensington.

DRIVER: Very good, sir.

TEMPLE enters and closes the taxi door.

TEMPLE: We can talk on the way to Luigi's, Doctor – if you've no objections.

KOHIMA: No, by all means.

The taxi starts up and drives away.

A moment.

KOHIMA: (*A hesitant manner*) I think you know why – why I wanted to see you, Mr Temple?

TEMPLE: Yes.

KOHIMA: I've made up my mind to tell you the truth – the whole truth about …

TEMPLE: About Mrs Trevelyan …

KOHIMA: Yes. (*It is not easy for him to tell his story*) Mr Temple, I don't quite know how to begin my story. All my life I've been listening to other people's, and now – for the first time – I – I – (*Quickly, almost as if he is collecting his thoughts*) Several years ago I met – and fell in love – with Mrs Trevelyan. She was a wonderful woman in those days, Mr Temple. So gay, so full of life. She had a keen, but of course an amateurish, interest in psychology – and after a little while I persuaded her to work for me as my private secretary. She was a nice person, Mr Temple, and I had great confidence in her. And then one morning I discovered …

TEMPLE: That she was passing information about your patients – confidential information – on to someone else?

146

KOHIMA: Yes! I was horrified! I just didn't know what to do! When I challenged her she simply broke down and confessed. (*A moment*) And then I heard the whole sordid story. She, in turn, was being blackmailed. Blackmailed into getting the information. Blackmailed by ALEX …

A pause.

TEMPLE: Dr Kohima, tell me, is Mrs Trevelyan a wealthy sort of person?

KOHIMA: Why, no! Why do you ask?

TEMPLE: I believe – or I have reason to believe – that she gave …

KOHIMA: She gave ALEX three thousand pounds. I gave her that money, Mr Temple. I had to. There was no alternative.

TEMPLE: You could have gone to the police.

KOHIMA: I know. But rightly or wrongly – I didn't.

A pause.

TEMPLE: Why are you telling me all this, Dr Kohima?

KOHIMA: Because you've got to believe me, Mr Temple, that Mrs Trevelyan is not ALEX!!!

FADE UP of music.
Music rises to a climax.

FADE DOWN of music.
FADE UP of a buzzer at the front door of a flat.
We hear the buzzer several times.
A door opens.

CARL: (*Surprised, quite pleasantly*) Why, hello, Temple!

TEMPLE: Hello, Lathom, I hope I haven't disturbed you!

CARL: No, of course you haven't. Come in!

Door closes.

TEMPLE: I say, I do hope I haven't got you out of bed.

147

CARL: No, of course not! As a matter of fact I was dozing in front of the fire. (*Suddenly*) Here, let me take your coat!

TEMPLE: Ah! That's what I call a fire!

CARL: What would you like to drink? Whisky – sherry – brandy – gin and lime – gin and ginger ale – gin and French – gin and Italian – dry Martini?

TEMPLE: No Port?

CARL: (*Laughing*) I'm afraid I'm right out of Port just at the moment.

TEMPLE: (*Quietly; significantly*) Lathom …

CARL: Yes?

TEMPLE: You were quite right.

CARL: Right? About what?

TEMPLE: About that girl. It was … the girl in brown.

CARL: Good Lord! (*Quickly*) Well – what did she say? Did she tell you why she's been following … (*He stops*) What is it? What's happened, Temple???!!!

TEMPLE: She's dead – murdered.

CARL: Mur – You mean that she was dead when you got to your house?

TEMPLE: Yes.

CARL: But this is incredible! Who was she, Temple?

TEMPLE: I don't know.

CARL: (*Surprised even further*) You don't know! But – but you must know! Didn't you search the body?

TEMPLE: No.

CARL: Why not?

TEMPLE: Because I think she'd already been searched – by Inspector Crane.

CARL: By Inspector Crane? But she couldn't have
           been unless he was already there when you
           arrived.
TEMPLE: He was. He apparently arrived at the flat just
           after the girl was murdered.
CARL: Did he see anyone?
TEMPLE: No.
CARL: But what was Crane doing at the flat?
TEMPLE: It seems he wanted to see me. He'd just missed
           us at Luigi's.
CARL: (*Thoughtfully*) How long have you known
           Crane?
TEMPLE: Oh, not very long. Why do you ask?
CARL: You don't think that he shot the girl?
TEMPLE: Why should he? Incidentally, how did you
           know that she was shot?
CARL: Why – why you said so!
TEMPLE: No – I said she'd been murdered.
CARL: Well – murdered – shot – it's the same thing.
TEMPLE: Not exactly the same. I mean, she might have
           been strangled – or stabbed – or poisoned even.
CARL: Yes. I suppose she might have been. I never
           thought of that. (*A laugh*) I say, look here, you
           don't think that I had anything to do with this
           business, do you?
TEMPLE: Well – had you?
CARL: Of course I hadn't!
TEMPLE: What happened after you left Luigi's? Did you
           come straight back here?
CARL: (*Not amused*) Yes, of course I did. But look
           here, don't ask me to prove it.
TEMPLE: Why not?
CARL: Well – no one saw me come in and since my
           housekeeper happens to be away … (*Suddenly,*
149

a happy thought) Ah! Ah! But I couldn't have done it, could I?

TEMPLE: What do you mean?

CARL: You left me at Luigi's! Now I ask you: how could I have got to your flat before you and Mrs Temple arrived?

TEMPLE: We had a puncture and, unfortunately, were delayed.

CARL: A puncture! That was bad luck.

TEMPLE: Well – I wouldn't exactly call it bad luck. There was glass right across the entrance to the mews – where I'd parked the car. It had obviously been put there.

CARL: You mean deliberately?

TEMPLE: Yes.

CARL: Temple, why – why did you come here tonight? Was it because you thought that I had something to do with this business …

TEMPLE: I came for two reasons, Lathom. Firstly: because I wanted you to know about the girl, and secondly because I think you ought to be warned.

CARL: (*Nervously*) Warned? Warned – about what?

TEMPLE: I have a feeling that ALEX isn't very favourably impressed by the fact that you consulted me.

CARL: ALEX! But Mrs Trevelyan is ALEX!

TEMPLE: Do you think that Mrs Trevelyan is ALEX?

CARL: No! No, I don't! I told Mrs Temple I didn't think that … (*Checking himself*) But Mrs Trevelyan turned up at Haybourne – for the three thousand pounds so surely … (*He is thinking: obviously alarmed*) Temple, if Mrs

150

Trevelyan isn't ALEX, then ALEX must know
that I – that I consulted you about the letter.

TEMPLE: Yes.

CARL: That's what you meant when you said I ought
            to be warned? That's what you meant, wasn't
            it?

TEMPLE: That's what I meant.

CARL: You think I'm in danger, don't you? (*On edge*)
            Don't you?

TEMPLE: Well …

CARL: Well?

TEMPLE: (*A warning, but in quite a friendly manner*)
            Well – I should certainly watch your step, Mr
            Lathom.

FADE UP of music.

Slow FADE DOWN of music.

A door opens.

SIR GRAHAM, STEVE and TEMPLE enter.

The door closes.

STEVE: Now there's no need to rush away, Sir Graham
            – I'm quite sure you'd like some coffee.

FORBES: Well, I really ought to be making a move, Steve
            …

TEMPLE: Nonsense! It's still quite early. Besides, you've
            got to smoke that cigar first! Tell Ricky about
            the coffee, darling.

STEVE: Yes, all right.

Door opens and closes.

FORBES: (*Settling down into the armchair*) Ah, thank
            you, Temple!

A pause.

151

TEMPLE: (*Thoughtfully, preparing a cigar*) It was a great pity about that girl – the girl in brown – wasn't it, Sir Graham?

FORBES: Yes. Did you know that she was an American?

TEMPLE: Yes … I thought she might be.

FORBES: You never actually saw her though, did you – not until …

TEMPLE: Not until that night, no.

FORBES: Carol … Reagan.

TEMPLE: Yes.

FORBES: Crane tells me that she was pretty well known in the States.

TEMPLE: Oh, very. She used to work with a man called Myers – Jeff Myers.

FORBES: Good gracious, I remember reading about Myers! He was with the F.B.I.

TEMPLE: For a while – yes. And then I believe he started up as a sort of – well – I suppose you might call him a private eye. Myers is a strange bird but he's got a pretty good reputation in America.

FORBES: What do you think happened that night, Temple? The night she came here?

TEMPLE: I don't know. She quite obviously came here with the intention of telling me something of importance.

FORBES: Have you any idea what it was?

TEMPLE: Yes, I think perhaps I have.

FORBES: When you telephoned this morning and invited me to dinner you said you'd received a letter …

TEMPLE: Yes, a letter I rather wanted you to see. It came by the first post. Here it is. Don't let Steve see it – I don't want her to be worried.

FORBES: It's from ALEX!

TEMPLE: Yes.

152

FORBES: (*Reading*) "If you value your life, Mr Temple –
Stop interfering! This is my first and last
warning! Stop interfering! ALEX!" This letter
was posted in Hampstead, I see.

TEMPLE: Yes. But it was typed on the usual machine –
the one at Canterbury.

FORBES: Temple, I'm glad you've confided in me –
about why you went down to the Waverley in
the first place – but …

TEMPLE: But what, Sir Graham?

FORBES: Well – do you think it was a good idea sending
that friend of yours down to Canterbury?

TEMPLE: You needn't have any qualms about Leo, Sir
Graham. He's pretty shrewd.

FORBES: M'm. When did he go down there?

TEMPLE: The day before yesterday.

FORBES: Well, I've got a feeling I ought to send
someone from the Yard – I mean – Bradley or
Crane. You see, Temple, the whole of this …

TEMPLE: No! Don't do that, Sir Graham, please! At least
– not yet.

FORBES: Have you heard from Brent?

TEMPLE: Yes, of course. We arranged to keep in touch.

FORBES: Well – what's happening?

TEMPLE: He said he found things most …

The door opens.

STEVE enters with a trolley.

TEMPLE: Ah, here we are!

STEVE: No, don't get up, Sir Graham! It's all right – I
can manage!

They move around slightly.

STEVE: Black or white?

FORBES: Er – black, please.

STEVE: Black, darling?

153

TEMPLE: Please. What would you like as a liqueur?

TEMPLE is interrupted by the telephone; it rings for a little while.

STEVE: That'll be for you, dear.

TEMPLE: Yes. I think it's from Canterbury, Sir Graham. Would you like to take the extension it's …

FORBES: Yes, I would, Temple!

TEMPLE: It's in the study – you know the way.

A moment.

The door opens.

TEMPLE lifts the receiver.

TEMPLE: (*On the phone*) Hello?

BRENT: (*On the other end of the line*) Hello …

TEMPLE: Hello – is that you, Leo?

BRENT: Yeah! Hello, Paul!

TEMPLE: (*A moment*) Well – how's things?

BRENT: Pretty dull! Say, I don't want to be fussy, Paul, but does anything ever happen down here?

TEMPLE: I thought you said this morning that things were getting warmer?

BRENT: That was this morning! There's been a deep depression over the district since then.

TEMPLE: You've seen Chester?

BRENT: Sure. I'm tailing him. Tailing him night and day. But he don't do anything except play golf and run the hotel. And he's not so hot on either. Say, Paul, are you sure you're not barking up the wrong tree?

TEMPLE: Quite sure, Leo. I think you'd better come back to Town.

BRENT: Sure. Suits me. I'll see you tomorrow. Goodbye, Paul!

TEMPLE: Goodbye.

TEMPLE replaces the receiver.

A moment.

STEVE: (*Noticing TEMPLE's expression*) What's the matter, darling? Has something happened?

The door opens.

FORBES returns.

TEMPLE: You heard ... all right ...?

FORBES: Yes – but quite frankly, Temple, I can't say I'm particularly impressed by your friend Mr Brent!

TEMPLE: That wasn't my friend Mr Brent.

FORBES: What do you mean?

TEMPLE: That wasn't Leo Brent!

STEVE: But, Paul, I heard the voice myself, I'm sure it was Leo.

TEMPLE: No! That wasn't Leo! I'm sure it wasn't! He kept calling me Paul all the time. Leo doesn't do that, darling! He's never done it! It's Temple! Always Temple! (*Quickly*) Steve, tell Ricky to pack a bag!

STEVE: Pack a bag? But we're not going down to Canterbury, are we? ...

TEMPLE: We are!

FORBES: Tonight?

TEMPLE: Tonight, Sir Graham!!!

FADE UP of music.

FADE DOWN of music.

FADE UP of the sound of a typewriter.

It stops.

THOMAS: Good evening, sir!

TEMPLE: Good evening. I think you have a reservation for me. I telephoned from London ...

THOMAS: Mr Temple?

TEMPLE: Yes.

155

THOMAS: Certainly, Mr Temple. Would you mind registering, sir? Good evening, madam.

STEVE: Good evening.

TEMPLE: Would it be possible for me to have a word with Mr Chester?

THOMAS: Mr Chester isn't here, sir – he's on holiday.

TEMPLE: Oh?

THOMAS: He left this afternoon, sir – about four o'clock. Is there anything I can do …?

TEMPLE: (*Dismissing the matter*) No, that's all right, thank you.

The sound of a key.

THOMAS: Room Thirty-Two, sir.

TEMPLE: Thank you. (*Suddenly, not surprised*) Oh, hello, Davis!

DAVIS: (*Surprised; but his manner is older and rather subdued*) Hello, Mr Temple – Mrs Temple – have you both just arrived?

TEMPLE: Yes. I thought we might bump into you.

STEVE: You told us that you were coming down here … (*Hesitating*) … Have you been ill, Mr Davis, since we last saw you?

DAVIS: Yes, I'm afraid I've been under the weather, Mrs Temple. Are you staying down here for long?

TEMPLE: Just for the one night, I think.

DAVIS: I see.

TEMPLE: Thirty-Two, you said?

THOMAS: Yes, sir. Room Thirty-Two.

DAVIS: (*Hesitantly*) We might meet tomorrow morning perhaps at breakfast?

TEMPLE: Yes. Yes, by all means. Ready, darling?

STEVE: Goodnight, Mr Davis!

DAVIS: Goodnight, Mrs Temple! I was out this afternoon when the post arrived and I was wondering if by any chance there was ... ...

Voice FADED.
FADE Scene.

FADE UP.

STEVE: We've passed Thirty-One so ... Oh, here we are, Paul! Thirty-Two ...

TEMPLE: Yes. (*Softly, rather urgently; opening the door with a key*) Steve, listen! I shan't be long! Wait in the room until the boy arrives with the luggage and then ...

STEVE: Darling, where are you going?

TEMPLE: I'm going down to Leo's room – it's on the next floor.

STEVE: Did he tell you the number?

TEMPLE: Yes – it's fourteen. I'll be back in two or three minutes. Now don't worry!

STEVE: (*Thoughtfully*) Well, I'm sure about one thing! You were quite right, darling. That couldn't have been Leo on the telephone tonight because if it was he'd have told you about Chester.

TEMPLE: Yes. (*Quickly*) Darling, here's the boy with the luggage! I shan't be long!

STEVE: Okay!

Quick FADE UP of music.

FADE DOWN of music.
A door opens and STEVE gives a sudden start of surprise.

STEVE: Oh!

TEMPLE: Sorry, darling.

The door closes.

STEVE: You did make me jump! (*Quickly*) Did you see Leo?

TEMPLE: No! … I found his room all right but there was no sign of Leo … When he didn't answer, I tried the door – and it wasn't locked … So I slipped in to have a quick look around …

STEVE: Did anyone see you?

TEMPLE: No. I was nearly caught coming out of the room but I managed to duck back in time … Anyway, you remember what Leo said at Luigi's? … It's all done by …

STEVE: (*Quickly*) "It's all done by mirrors"! You mean he left a note for you behind the dressing table mirror?

TEMPLE: Yes.

STEVE: What does it say?

TEMPLE: I haven't had a chance to read it yet. (*A sigh; getting his breath*) Gosh, I'm out of breath! Now let's see … (*Rips open the note: reads slowly*) "Dear Temple – This is just in case I can't phone you tonight as arranged. This morning Chester paid a visit …" What's that word, darling?

STEVE: … (*Reading*) … "to Claywood Mill. I have reason to believe that he is going there again this afternoon. The Mill is supposed to be derelict but I have a feeling it is here that …" What's that?

TEMPLE: (*Reading*) … "It is here that Chester contacts ALEX. The Mill is about sixteen miles from Faversham and four from Moondale. It stands by the side of a wood near…" Claywood Milll!!!! Steve! Do you remember that night – the night we found Spider Williams?

158

STEVE: Yes …

TEMPLE: Before we got back onto the main road we passed a wood – on the left-hand side. There was a Mill – not far from the wood. An old sort of Mill with a broken-down water wheel!

STEVE: Yes, I remember! Spider said he saw ALEX …

TEMPLE: So ALEX must have been waiting for us! He must have been at the Mill waiting until the accident happened. (*He hesitates*)

STEVE: Paul, what is it?

TEMPLE: (*His thoughts elsewhere*) Did you pack a torch, darling?

STEVE: (*A little surprised*) Yes. There's one here and there's a big one in the car.

TEMPLE: Good. Get your coat, dear.

STEVE: Where are we going?

TEMPLE: Where do you think we're going – the Isle of Man?

FADE UP of music.

FADE DOWN of music.

FADE UP of the sound of an outdoor scene; we are at Claywood Mill.

Very faintly, and in the distance, the sound of a church clock can be heard chiming the half-hour.

Somewhere across country, a dog can be heard barking. The sound of birds.

The quick rustle of wind in the trees.

TEMPLE and STEVE can be heard approaching.

STEVE: Gosh, my shoes are muddy!

TEMPLE: Thank goodness you had the sense to put some low heels on, Steve!

STEVE: This place is certainly derelict!

TEMPLE: Yes … It doesn't look as if it's been used for ages!

STEVE: Where's the entrance?

TEMPLE: I don't know … Unless … Oh, there it is!

STEVE: Oh, dear!

TEMPLE: What's the matter?

STEVE: You've got to walk across the water to get to it.

TEMPLE: Well – there's a bridge!

STEVE: (*With a nervous little laugh*) If you can call it a bridge!

TEMPLE: Give me your hand!

STEVE: Go slowly, darling –I'm always nervous of this sort of thing.

TEMPLE: Nonsense – it's as safe as houses …

TEMPLE steps onto the wooden plank across the water.

The bridge commences to creak.

TEMPLE: … I hope! Now take it steady – don't rush things …

STEVE: I haven't the slightest intention of – rushing things.

A pause.

The bridge continues to creak.

TEMPLE: We're halfway across already!

STEVE: Yes, well don't speak too …

A pebble falls into the water with a sudden plop.

STEVE: What was that?

TEMPLE: (*Amused*) It's all right, I only kicked a pebble into the water.

The bridge continues to creak, then suddenly:

STEVE: (*With relief*) Oh! We're across!

TEMPLE: Yes – but we've still got to get back!

STEVE: You beast!

TEMPLE: This is a pretty grim looking place at close quarters, isn't it?

STEVE: It's more like an old castle than a mill ... The water wheel doesn't look as if it's been used for centuries!

TEMPLE: I'm not so sure about that! Hold my hand, darling – I want to lean across ... Hold tight ... (*A moment; relaxing*) Okay!

STEVE: Well?

TEMPLE: The wheel's been used – and fairly recently too, if I'm any judge. There's oil right across the crankshaft.

STEVE: What on earth could it have been used for?

TEMPLE: I don't know. There seems to be some sort of a pump attached to it. Let's take a look inside.

A moment.

The door creaks open; a heavy wooden door.

TEMPLE: Wait a moment! Don't come in for a second! Stay where you are, darling!

TEMPLE pushes the door further open.

A pause.

STEVE: (*Behind TEMPLE; waiting*) Well? (*A moment*) Can you see anything?

TEMPLE: No, the place certainly looks deserted ... Okay, Steve ... I've got hold of the door!

The door opens wider, then closes.

STEVE: Smells awfully musty, doesn't it?

TEMPLE: Yes – it's damp.

Pause.

STEVE: It's not quite so big inside as I imagined ...

TEMPLE: No. That looks like a loft over there but I can't see any means of getting up ... Steve, listen!

STEVE: What is it?

TEMPLE: Listen!!

Beneath them, we hear the muffled voice of LEO BRENT; he sounds weak and exhausted.

BRENT: Help! – Help! – Help! – Let me out of here! …
            Can you hear me? Help! Help! …
STEVE: It's Leo Brent!
TEMPLE: (*Shouting*) Leo! Leo, where are you? It's
            Temple! Where are you!!!?
BRENT: (*Faintly, from beneath them*) Temple! I can't
            get up. I've broken my leg!
TEMPLE: Where are you? Where are you, Leo???
BRENT: I'm in the basement. There's a trap door,
            Temple … You'll see it … in the middle of the
            floor!
TEMPLE: Flash that light! Flash it over here, darling!
STEVE: There it is – you can see the iron ring …
TEMPLE: Yes!

TEMPLE commences to pull open the trap door.

BRENT: Temple?
TEMPLE: Where are you, Leo?
BRENT: I'm over in the corner – flash your torch down
            a little and over to the right.
STEVE: Oh! There he is, Paul!
TEMPLE: By Timothy, you look as if you've caught a
            packet!
BRENT: You're telling me! I've been shouting my guts
            out for the last six hours! (*Wincing with pain*)
            Gosh – this leg's giving me hell!
TEMPLE: I'm coming down, Leo!
BRENT: Be careful – it's only a wooden ladder!
TEMPLE: You stay here, Steve!
BRENT: Watch your step, Temple!
STEVE: Be careful, darling!

*TEMPLE slowly descends the wooden ladder into the
basement.*

TEMPLE: That leg looks pretty bad, Leo! Is it broken?

162

BRENT: Yeah, I'm afraid so. But, boy, am I glad to see you! Talk about a miracle! I was just about to give up all hope of ever ... But, say, how come you got wise to this place anyway?

TEMPLE: Well, when I got your note ...

BRENT: What note?

TEMPLE: The note you stuck behind the mirror on your dressing table.

BRENT: I didn't write any note!

TEMPLE: You didn't? Well, somebody did, and planted it behind the mirror – and deliberately left the Yale catch up so that I could get into your room.

At this moment STEVE utters the first of a series of shrieks and commences to struggle.

BRENT: TEMPLE!!!!

TEMPLE: (*Alarmed*) Steve, what is it?

There is a bang; it is the closing of the trap door.

BRENT: My God, Temple! They've closed the trap!!!

TEMPLE rushes up the ladder and attempts to force open the door.

BRENT: Can't you open it!!!!

TEMPLE: No, it won't move!

BRENT: (*Wildly and in pain*) My God, if only I could get up that ... (*In pain*) Oh!!!!

STEVE is screaming for help and in desperation TEMPLE starts to beat against the trap door.

TEMPLE: Steve! Steve!

Suddenly the whir of a dynamo is heard and the water wheel commences to turn; it quickly gathers momentum.

BRENT: Temple, what's that?

TEMPLE: It's the wheel!!!!

BRENT: The water wheel! What's the idea? What in hell is the idea? What are they up to?

163

TEMPLE: I don't know … I …

BRENT: Look! Temple, they're going to flood the place!! They're pumping water into the cellar!!

Water can be heard rushing into the cellar; the pressure quickly increases.

TEMPLE: (*Beating on the trap door*) We've got to get out of here!

BRENT: If we don't – then by God we're trapped!

TEMPLE: Steve! STEVE!!

TEMPLE continues to throw his weight against the trap door.

FADE UP of TEMPLE banging against the trap door as the water rushes into the cellar.

FADE UP of closing music.

END OF EPISODE SEVEN

EPISODE EIGHT

INTRODUCING ALEX

OPEN TO: *LEO BRENT's voice.*

BRENT: Temple, what's that?

TEMPLE: It's the wheel!!

BRENT: The water wheel! What's the idea? What in hell is the idea? What are they up to?

TEMPLE: I don't know.

BRENT: Look! Temple, they're going to flood the place!! They're pumping water into the cellar!!

Water can be heard rushing into the cellar; the pressure quickly increases.

TEMPLE: (*Beating on the trap door*) We've got to get out of here!

BRENT: If we don't – then by God we're trapped!

TEMPLE: Steve! STEVE!!

TEMPLE continues to throw his weight against the trap.

TEMPLE: We'll never be able to force this trapdoor …

BRENT: There's a window over on the left but – there's a piece of sacking across it …

TEMPLE: Oh, yes! But this is no use – we'll never be able to get out of this!

TEMPLE breaks the window.

BRENT: Say, this is one heck of a situation, we can't go …

TEMPLE: I'll have to move you up the ladder, Leo. Do you think you can hold on if I manage to lift you?

BRENT: Sure – I can hold on, but for how long?

TEMPLE: Well, the way things are going at the moment I should think this place will be flooded out in …

In the distance we hear SIR GRAHAM's voice.

TEMPLE: Listen!

BRENT: What? (*A moment*) It's the water you can hear!

TEMPLE: No!! By Timothy! I do believe it's Forbes!!!! (*Shouting*) Sir Graham!!!!

167

Suddenly they can hear voices.

BRENT: Gee, you're right!! There's a couple of guys up there unless I'm going screwy!!!!

The trap door is thrown open.

TEMPLE: Sir Graham!!

FORBES: I'm throwing a rope down …

TEMPLE: Where's Steve?

FORBES: Steve's all right … Get hold of the rope! Quickly!!

TEMPLE: There's a rope coming down, Leo …

BRENT: That's okay – I'll make it …

FORBES: You'll have to be quick, Temple!!

TEMPLE: Get hold of the rope, Leo! Don't pull! Not yet, Sir Graham!

FADE UP of water and the sound of the waterwheel.

FORBES: Are you ready?

TEMPLE: Ready, Leo?

BRENT: Yeah, but take it easy, brother!

TEMPLE: Okay … Pull now, Sir Graham!!

FORBES is pulling on the rope: hoisting BRENT.

TEMPLE: (*Straining*) Okay?

BRENT: (*Straining and in pain*) Yeah – we'll make it … We'll make it!!!!

TEMPLE: Take it steady, Leo … That's it … That's it … Now give me your hand … That's it!!! All right, Sir Graham – I've got him!!

Quick FADE UP of effects and CROSS FADE into music.

Music FADES DOWN and FADE UP of a car ticking over: in the distant background the waterwheel can still be heard.

STEVE: … I was watching you go down into the cellar, Paul, when suddenly someone came up behind me and put their hand over my face. I screamed –

168

TEMPLE: We heard you, darling.

BRENT: Did you see the man, Mrs Temple?

STEVE: No, I'm afraid I didn't. I must have been almost in a faint by the time Inspector Crane arrived.

TEMPLE: Is Crane here?

FORBES: Yes – but he's on the lookout for our old friend Davis.

TEMPLE: Davis?

FORBES: Yes – if it hadn't been for him we never should have found this place.

TEMPLE: Well – if it comes to that how did you find it?

FORBES: After you left Town I suddenly made up my mind to ignore your advice and bring Crane down here. As soon as we arrived at the Waverley we bumped bang-slap into Davis. He was just leaving and seemed to me to be in a pretty first-class hurry. We tailed him – and – well – here we are.

TEMPLE: I see.

STEVE: (*Suddenly*) Here's Inspector Crane, darling!

CRANE arrives: breathless.

CRANE: Davis has given me the slip I'm afraid, sir. There's no sign of him. But we've picked up Chester. Look here, Temple, do you reckon this Welsh fellow Wilfred Davis is ALEX or …

TEMPLE: Or what, Inspector?

CRANE: Well, I always thought it was Dr Kohima, but …

TEMPLE: I know you did, Inspector.

CRANE: …But now … (*Bluntly*) Temple, do you know who ALEX really is?

FORBES: Of course Temple doesn't know who he is.

TEMPLE: Yes, Inspector – I know.

FORBES: What?!!

169

STEVE: Darling, do you know what you're saying?

BRENT: This is no time for ribbing us …

TEMPLE: I'm not joking, Leo.

FORBES: Temple, are you serious?

TEMPLE: Well, if I'm not joking I must be serious, mustn't I, Sir Graham? Yes, I know the identity of ALEX. I've suspected it for quite some time. Last night – I knew for certain that I was right.

CRANE: (*Bluntly*) Well, then – who is ALEX?

TEMPLE: (*Evasively*) Supposing you meet me at my flat –

CRANE: WHO – IS – ALEX?

A moment.

TEMPLE: You'd like to meet him, Inspector?

CRANE: Like to … I most certainly would!

TEMPLE: Very well, I'll introduce you.

CRANE: When?

FORBES: Yes, when, Temple?

TEMPLE: Tomorrow night …

STEVE: Darling!

CRANE: Where?

TEMPLE: At my house, Inspector. Will eight o'clock be convenient?

CRANE: Quite convenient!

TEMPLE: Then it's a date, Inspector. It's a date …

FADE UP of music.

FADE DOWN of music.

TEMPLE is whistling to himself.

STEVE: You look very pleased with yourself!

TEMPLE: I feel very pleased with myself, Steve!

STEVE: Yes, well, your hair looks very nice, darling – there's no need to start brushing it all over again.

170

There is a knock on the door and the door opens.

RICKY: Excuse me, sir!

TEMPLE: Yes, what is it, Ricky?

RICKY: Shall you be wanting me any more this evening, sir?

TEMPLE: Any more?

STEVE: Oh – I forgot to tell you – it's Ricky's night out.

TEMPLE: Oh, Lord!

RICKY: Did you wish me to stay in tonight, sir?

TEMPLE: Well, I'm rather afraid I did, Ricky …

RICKY: Okay! That's all right. I stay.

TEMPLE: Oh – er – well – thanks very much.

RICKY: Thank you, Mr Temple! (*Suddenly, remembering*) Oh, excuse me! I forget! Mr Carl Lathom, Sir Graham Forbes and Inspector Crane have arrived, sir.

TEMPLE: Oh, have they? Splendid! Come on, Steve!

STEVE: Mr Lathom! Does that mean …?

TEMPLE: It probably means he's helping himself to a very good dose of whisky. Come along, darling, before he drinks the bottle.

The door opens.

FADE UP of voices: SIR GRAHAM, CARL LATHOM and INSPECTOR CRANE.

CRANE: … (*On his dignity*) Ah, here's Mr Temple! Now look here, Temple, you told me that …

TEMPLE: (*Dominating the scene*) Hello, Inspector! Good gracious, haven't you helped yourself to a drink yet? Ah, hello, Lathom! You got my note all right? (*He is moving glasses*)

CARL: Yes, thank you, Temple. But for the life of me … Oh, good evening, Mrs Temple!

FORBES: Hello, Steve!

171

STEVE: Hello, Sir Graham! Good evening, Mr
                Lathom … Inspector …
CRANE: (*Thawing slightly*) Good evening, Mrs
                Temple. I trust you're feeling none the
                worse for your experience at Claywood
                Mill?

The flat buzzer can be heard.

STEVE: No, I'm feeling quite myself … Paul,
                there's someone at the door!
TEMPLE: (*Shaking a cocktail shaker*) Oh! Just finish
                mixing this cocktail, darling.
STEVE: Oh, dear! I'm … not very good at this sort
                of thing I'm afraid, do you think you could
                manage it, Inspector, or …
CRANE: Er – well …
CARL: Allow me, Mrs Temple! (*Taking the
                shaker; obviously experienced*)
FORBES: (*Pleasantly*) You seem quite an expert, Mr
                Lathom.
CARL: (*Over emphasised*) The sign of a mis-spent
                youth!

They laugh.

FADE across to the opening of the front door.
*FORBES, LATHOM, STEVE and the INSPECTOR still
produce a background of conversation.*

TEMPLE: Ah, Mrs Trevelyan! Oh – good evening,
                Dr Kohima!
KOHIMA: I'm afraid we're rather late, Mr Temple …
TEMPLE: No! Not at all! Come in, Mrs Trevelyan!

The door closes.

TEMPLE: Let me take your hat, Doctor.

TREVELYAN: (*Nervously, on edge*) What is it you wanted to see us about, Mr Temple? When I got your message I ...

KOHIMA: (*Interrupting MRS TREVELYAN: suddenly*) Why ... is that Sir Graham Forbes I can hear, and – Inspector Crane ...?

TEMPLE: Yes ...

KOHIMA: But I thought you wanted to have a confidential chat with Mrs Trevelyan and myself ...

TREVELYAN: (*Suddenly; amazed*) Why, that's Mr Lathom!

KOHIMA: Lathom?

TEMPLE: Yes – that's Mr Lathom.

KOHIMA: But why on earth should ...

TEMPLE: (*Laughing*) Come along, Doctor ...

A door opens.

FADE UP of FORBES, STEVE, CRANE and LATHOM. As they see DR KOHIMA and MRS TREVELYAN their voices die down into an astonished silence.

LATHOM: Dr Kohima!

CRANE: Mrs Trevelyan! (*Surprised and irritated*) What is this, Temple – a party or something?

TEMPLE: Hardly a party, Inspector! Let's say a family gathering! (*Suddenly; brightly*) Would you like a drink, Mrs Trevelyan ...

TREVELYAN: No, thank you, Mr Temple.

TEMPLE: Dr Kohima?

KOHIMA: (*Suspiciously*) No, sir ...

TEMPLE: Well, er, you don't mind if I do? Ah! Thank you, Mr Lathom!

The door bell can be heard.

TEMPLE:	Your very good health … Excuse me!

A moment.

KOHIMA:	(*Nervously*) Sir Graham, why did Mr Temple send for us like this!? What exactly are we doing here?
CARL:	Yes … Yes, by Jove, what are we doing here? (*Puzzled*) I simply got a note from Temple asking me to pop in and see him at eight o'clock tonight …
CRANE:	I think I know why <u>you</u> are here, Dr Kohima …
KOHIMA:	Indeed?
FORBES:	Inspector Crane asked Temple if he knew the identity of ALEX. Temple's reply was to the effect that …

In the hall the clock has started to chime the hour.

CRANE:	Not only did he know the identity of ALEX but that he would introduce me to ALEX … here … tonight … at … eight o'clock!!!!

There is a general gasp of astonishment from KOHIMA, LATHOM and MRS TREVELYAN.

The door opens.

FADE UP of the clock on the last chimes – and TEMPLE returns with WILFRED DAVIS.

The clock stops chiming as STEVE speaks.

STEVE:	Why, hello, Mr Davis!
DAVIS:	(*Pleasantly*) We meet again, Mrs Temple!
TEMPLE:	(*Glibly*) I don't know whether you know … Sir Graham Forbes … Mrs Trevelyan … Dr Kohima … Carl Lathom … Inspector Crane …
DAVIS:	I'm very pleased to meet you all, I'm sure …

174

FORBES: (*Suddenly, suspiciously*) Mr Davis, you were at Canterbury last night, staying at the …

TEMPLE: (*Deliberately interrupting FORBES*) Would you like a drink, Davis? By Timothy, I know I would.

STEVE: You've got one in your hand, darling!

TEMPLE: Oh, so I have! (*Laughing*) Well – here's to crime! Oh – perhaps I shouldn't have said that! Down the hatch! (*He drinks*)

FORBES: Temple, I don't want to seem impatient but …

A door opens.

STEVE: What is it, Ricky?

RICKY: So sorry. So sorry to interrupt but the drawing room is quite ready now, sir.

TEMPLE: Ah, splendid! Now listen, everybody! There's a very pleasant fire in the drawing room and a number of very comfortable chairs. I want you all to go in there and make yourselves as comfortable as possible, because … (*He hesitates*)

CRANE: Because … <u>what</u> … Mr Temple?!

TEMPLE: Because I'm going to keep my promise, Inspector … (*Seriously*) … and introduce you to ALEX.

Quick flourish of music.
Music dies down.

FADE UP of slight conversation which dies down as PAUL TEMPLE speaks.

TEMPLE: Ah, that's better … I should sit over in the corner, Dr Kohima … Well, I expect you are all … It's all right, Ricky, you needn't go!

RICKY: You want me to stay, Mr Temple?

TEMPLE:	Yes. (*A moment; the flippancy has departed: he is serious*) Well, I expect you're all – with the exception of Sir Graham – wondering why exactly I invited you here this evening. Well, I'll tell you. Several years ago when I investigated a case, I took the liberty of inviting to my home all the possible suspects. Tonight I have followed – almost identically – the same procedure.
KOHIMA:	Mr Temple, you surely don't consider that I'm a possible suspect!
TEMPLE:	Inspector Crane does, Doctor – don't you, Inspector?

KOHIMA stirs.

CRANE:	(*Faintly irritated*) Now look here, Temple, it's …
TREVELYAN:	Mr Temple! … Do you mean that ALEX is here … in this room … that he's actually … one of us?

A tense pause.

TEMPLE:	That's precisely what I do mean, Mrs Trevelyan.

General astonishment.

CARL:	Forgive me saying so, but I think you owe us an explanation.
TEMPLE:	Of course I owe you an explanation, Lathom – I intend to give you one! But let me begin at the beginning and let me, in fact, start with … Suspect number one …
DAVIS:	(*Sing-song; suggestion of a smile*) Mrs Trevelyan …

TEMPLE: (*A note of amusement*) Oh, no, Mr Davis. Suspect number one! ... Wilfred Davis Esquire, alias Mr Cartwright, alias ... (*Is he going to say ALEX?*) ... Jeff Myers!!!!

FORBES: (*Astonished*) Jeff Myers!!!!

DAVIS: (*Laughing and completely dropping his Welsh accent*) You seem surprised, Sir Graham!

CRANE: Look here, Temple, are you trying to tell us that this man Davis is really ...

DAVIS: My name is Myers – Jeff Myers. Late of the Federal Bureau of Investigation. I came over to this country three months ago at the personal request of ...

STEVE: (*Astonished*) Your accent, Mr Davis!

DAVIS: Accent? (*Laughing, with his fake Welsh accent*) Oh, Lordy, now if it's a Welsh accent you want, Mrs Temple, I shall be only too happy to oblige, but ... (*Dropping the accent; seriously*) just at the moment I think we'll dispense with it. I came to this country at the personal request of Sir Ernest Cranbury.

STEVE: Sir Ernest Cranbury!

CARL: (*Surprised*) But surely that was the man who was murdered – the man on the discussion programme – the man who fell dead the night ...

TEMPLE: The night that Dr Kohima's car very nearly forced Steve and myself onto the pavement.

FORBES: Mr Davis, er – Myers, if what you say is true then ... why did Sir Ernest Cranbury send for you?

KOHIMA: Surely, you don't have to look very far for the answer to that question, Sir Graham?

FORBES: (*Rudely*) No.

KOHIMA:	Sir Ernest sent for Myers for precisely the same reason that you sent for Paul Temple. To catch ALEX. Correct me if I'm – er – mistaken, Mr Temple?
TEMPLE:	No, you're – not mistaken, Dr Kohima. Mr Myers has a reputation in America – a reputation for investigating cases of a strictly confidential nature. So far as Sir Ernest was concerned this case was strictly confidential.
CRANE:	(*Slowly*) Mr Myers, tell me – did you investigate this case alone …?
DAVIS:	No, I had a partner. A girl.
TEMPLE:	A girl called Carol Reagan. Known to us, Inspector, as – the girl in brown …
STEVE:	The girl in brown!
CARL:	You mean to say that the girl who followed me – the girl that followed Mrs Temple was …
CRANE:	(*A note of sarcasm*) Was nothing more or less than an amateur detective!
TEMPLE:	Hardly an amateur, Inspector. Carol Reagan was an extremely intelligent and a very courageous woman.
STEVE:	But why did she follow me, the night we went to Marshall House Terrace?
DAVIS:	We knew that from the moment Temple decided to investigate the case you would be in danger, and we wanted to make certain that what happened to Norma Rice shouldn't happen to you, Mrs Temple.
TREVELYAN:	Norma Rice? That was the girl on the railway train, the girl that … (*She stops; quietly, on edge*) You found my name

178

	written in the back of a diary belonging to Norma Rice, didn't you?
FORBES:	Not only in the back of a diary, Mrs Trevelyan, but also on a visiting card – a card belonging to Richard East.
TREVELYAN:	(*Tensely*) Do you think I murdered Norma Rice, Mr Temple? Do you think I murdered ... Richard East ...?
TEMPLE:	I know you <u>didn't</u>, Mrs Trevelyan!
CRANE:	How do you know, Mr Temple!!!?
TEMPLE:	Because they were murdered by ALEX, Inspector, and Mrs Trevelyan is NOT ... ALEX!!!

There is a quick sigh of relief from MRS TREVELYAN and a sudden, faintly astonished reaction from the others – excepting Dr KOHIMA.

CRANE:	Well, if Mrs Trevelyan isn't ALEX, Mr Temple, perhaps you wouldn't mind explaining exactly how she fits into the picture?
TEMPLE:	I shall be delighted, Inspector. (*A moment*) Several months ago ALEX hit upon the idea of blackmailing Mrs Trevelyan into supplying him with information about ...
FORBES:	About certain of Dr Kohima's patients!
TEMPLE:	Exactly, Sir Graham. ALEX knew that a psychiatrist gets information of an extremely confidential nature. At first, out of a sense of loyalty to Dr Kohima, Mrs Trevelyan refused to obey the instructions she received from ALEX. But ALEX was determined to carry out his plan and in order to frighten Mrs Trevelyan he ...
CARL:	He made it look as if she was ALEX!

179

TEMPLE:	Exactly, Lathom! You see, ALEX didn't only blackmail people for money – don't labour under that illusion. He had a carefully organised plan of campaign. ALEX blackmailed people into doing certain things – which ultimately would lead to – higher stakes. Frank Chester, for instance, at the Waverley Hotel, was completely under his thumb; so was Mrs Trevelyan, and so for that matter was Dr Kohima.
CARL:	Dr Kohima!
TEMPLE:	Yes. Although ALEX obtained the necessary information from Mrs Trevelyan he wasn't content with that – Oh, no! – He started to blackmail Dr Kohima.
CARL:	But look here, Temple, are you trying to tell us that ALEX blackmailed Mrs Trevelyan into turning up at Haybourne and into almost confessing …
TEMPLE:	Into almost confessing that she was ALEX. Yes, Mr Lathom.
STEVE:	But how could he do that, darling? Surely Mrs Trevelyan wouldn't go so far as …
TEMPLE:	Mrs Trevelyan was in love – and still is – with Dr Kohima. ALEX threatened to completely ruin Kohima unless …
FORBES:	By George, yes! By George, I see it! ALEX had already started to throw suspicion onto Kohima by planting the pencil by the body of James Barton.
TEMPLE:	He told Mrs Trevelyan that if she didn't confess to being ALEX he would…

TREVELYAN: (*With intense emotion*) It's true! Every word of it – it's true!!!

KOHIMA: Yes … it's true! He made me give him the ticket for my car that night … the night that you and Mrs Temple …

TEMPLE: Yes, I know, Dr Kohima …

KOHIMA: But when he made Barbara turn up at Haybourne – when he attempted …

TEMPLE: He overstepped the mark! You didn't mind paying him money – you didn't even stop at giving him information when it was necessary – but when he attempted to blackmail Mrs Trevelyan into confessing that she was ALEX … (*Chuckles*) … that was just too much of a good thing, wasn't it, Doctor? You can lead a horse to water but you can't make him drink!

CRANE: (*Quickly*) But look here, Temple, if Davis isn't ALEX, if Mrs Trevelyan isn't ALEX, and if Dr Kohima isn't ALEX …

FORBES: (*Equally surprised*) There are only two suspects left …

CRANE: Mr Lathom and … Ricky!

TEMPLE: And, of course, yourself, Inspector …

Another murmur of surprise.

CRANE: But – but surely you don't suspect me, Mr Temple?

TEMPLE: I did, Inspector, but … I … don't any longer …

RICKY: (*After a moment; nervously*) Please … don't … look at me, Mr Temple …

TEMPLE: I'm not looking at you, Ricky.

A tiny pause.

TEMPLE: I'm looking at Mr Lathom …

181

A stir of surprise, and then LATHOM commences to laugh.

CARL: Temple, you're not seriously suggesting that I'm ALEX are you, because …

TEMPLE: Because what?

CARL: Because, the idea's too stupid for words! Why good heavens, Temple, you know yourself that I received a letter from ALEX demanding …

TEMPLE: Demanding three thousand pounds. But what precisely does that prove?

CARL: Why, it proves that I'm not ALEX!

TEMPLE: Oh, no it doesn't. If anything it merely proves that you wanted to direct any possible suspicion away from yourself and onto Mrs Trevelyan.

STEVE: But, darling, what about the information about Cairo …

TEMPLE: What information about Cairo? The Cairo story of Mr Lathom's was sheer nonsense – a purely fictitious story to make us believe that …

CARL: I say, just a minute! Are you suggesting that I blackmailed Mrs Trevelyan into …

TEMPLE: I'm suggesting that you blackmailed not only Mrs Trevelyan, Mr Lathom – but literally hundreds and hundreds of other people!

CARL: Really? Now that's what I call a theory! Go on, Temple! I'm most intrigued.

TEMPLE: I thought you would be. Shall I tell you why you went to Dr Kohima's, Mr Lathom?

CARL: Please do …

TEMPLE: (*Quickly and with authority*) You went to Dr Kohima's to get the information you required – <u>not</u> because you were under the impression that you were suffering from hallucinations!

KOHIMA: (*Nervously*) That's true … that's true, Mr Temple, only …

182

CARL: Be quiet!!!

TEMPLE: You were being followed all right, Lathom –
            but at first you couldn't make head or tail of it.
            You didn't know who the girl was or what she
            wanted.

DAVIS: Carol suspected you, Lathom – right from the
            very beginning she suspected you.

TEMPLE: But she couldn't prove anything …

CARL: Can you prove anything, Mr Temple?!!!!

A tense moment.

TEMPLE: Lathom, do you remember that night … the
            night you went to Luigi's?

CARL: Of course I remember, why …

TEMPLE: You overheard me tell Steve what Leo Brent
            meant when he said it was all done by mirrors.
            That's how you were able to pull that trick on
            me at Canterbury.

CARL: Yes – you fell for it rather nicely, didn't you?

TEMPLE: I – I regret to say I fell for it rather nicely.
            However, we all make mistakes, Mr Lathom.

A moment.

TEMPLE: You made rather a beauty.

CARL: What do you mean?

TEMPLE: When Ricky turned up at Luigi's and asked you
            to deliver a message to me – you realised
            immediately that Carol Reagan was waiting to
            see me, and you knew that at last – at long last
            – you had an opportunity of putting an end to
            her investigations. Before delivering Ricky's
            message you went outside and planted glass in
            front of my car, then – and only then – you
            returned to Luigi's and delivered the message.
            When Steve and I left Luigi's you – because of
            the puncture – had a flying start on us. When

183

	we arrived at the flat the girl was already dead …
FORBES:	Go on, Temple …
TEMPLE:	Later that night I paid you a visit, Lathom, and it was then … that you made rather a stupid mistake.
CARL:	Oh, you mean that I referred to the fact that the girl had been shot when actually I was only supposed to know that she'd been murdered.
TEMPLE:	No. That's not what I'm referring to.
CARL:	Then what are you referring to?
TEMPLE:	Don't you remember? When I arrived at the flat you asked me to have a drink. You offered me whisky – sherry – brandy – gin and lime – gin and ginger ale" … And I said: "No Port?" … And you said, Mr Lathom … "I'm afraid I'm right out of Port just at the moment" …

A pause.

CARL:	Well – what are you getting at?
TEMPLE:	Mr Lathom, why didn't you have any Port? You bought a bottle at Luigi's quite early in the evening. I went back to Luigi's that night, before I called at your flat, and I made enquiries. If, as you said, you went straight back to the flat you must have had a bottle of Port … unless …
CARL:	(*Uncertain of himself; tensely*) Unless … what?
TEMPLE:	Unless – you – deliberately – smashed – it – outside of Luigi's and put the glass across the entrance to the mews where my car was parked.
CARL:	(*Completely losing control of himself*) Why … you clever bastard!

LATHOM overturns the table; STEVE screams; there is general consternation.

STEVE:	Look out, darling!!!! He's got a revolver!!!!
CARL:	Stand back! Stand back!! If anyone moves – I warn you – I'll … (*With menace*) … You heard me, Sir Graham!!!!
TEMPLE:	Now look here, Lathom, if you think …
CARL:	Temple, if you don't mind I'll do the talking for a change … (*He chuckles*) … And I think you'll find it interesting, my friend.
TREVELYAN:	(*Softly; tensely*) He's crazy! The man's mad!

CARL continues to chuckle.

STEVE:	Don't – don't move, darling …
CARL:	Don't worry, he won't move, Mrs Temple, not until he's heard what I've got to say …
TEMPLE:	What have you got to say, Lathom?
CARL:	Temple, do you know what killed Sir Ernest Cranbury? What killed Norma Rice?
TEMPLE:	Yes, they were poisoned.
CARL:	That's right – they were poisoned by a delayed action poison, my friend.

A moment.

FORBES:	Well?

CARL chuckles.

CRANE:	(*Angrily*) What are you getting at?
CARL:	(*Amused*) Don't you know what I'm getting at, Inspector?
CRANE:	I'm damned if I do!!!!
CARL:	(*Fiercely; a complete change*) Then I'll tell you!!!! I'll tell you, Inspector!!!! Ten minutes ago I mixed Temple a drink. You

	saw me do it, you were standing next to me, but what you didn't see …
CRANE:	My God!
STEVE:	You mean you put something into that drink – you deliberately put …
FORBES:	Delayed action poison!
CARL:	Exactly, Sir Graham!
STEVE:	Oh darling!
TREVELYAN:	Oh!
CARL:	You fools! You didn't think I'd fall for second-rate theories without a trick up my sleeve, did you? You didn't think that ALEX would … (*Sharply; tensely*) Don't move!! One move, Dr Kohima, and I'll fire ….
TEMPLE:	(*Quietly, but immediately drawing attention to himself*) Mr Lathom, do you remember what happened – when you gave me that drink?
CARL:	(*A moment*) What do you mean?
TEMPLE:	I lifted the glass up, said "Your very good health" … then changed my mind and went out into the hall to let in Mr Davis.
CARL:	(*Very sure of himself*) But when you came back into the room …
TEMPLE:	I'd already disposed of your drink, by pouring it down the kitchen sink. The glass was filled with water!
STEVE:	(*With intense relief*) Oh, Paul, I …
CARL:	(*Furiously*) Why you …
FORBES:	Look out, Temple!!!!
CRANE:	Look out, sir!!!!

There is a revolver shot; a shriek from STEVE; the smashing of a vase and a sudden moan from LATHOM.

186

FORBES: (*Breathlessly*) Temple, are you all right?

TEMPLE: I'm all right! What – what did you hit him with, Ricky?

RICKY: (*Misunderstanding*) The vase, sir …

CRANE: And a jolly good shot too, Ricky. By George if you hadn't caught him just at that moment …

RICKY: (*Apologetically*) Yes, but I'm so sorry – so sorry about the vase, Mrs Temple.

STEVE: Sorry!!!!

TEMPLE: My dear Ricky, we're delighted, I'm tickled to death!

RICKY: Oh! Thank you. Thank you, Mr Temple!

TEMPLE: No. No … Thank <u>you</u>, Ricky! I never could stand that vase!

FADE UP of music.

Slow FADE DOWN.

TEMPLE is enjoying his afternoon tea.

TEMPLE: M'm – these scones are delicious, Steve – I really …

STEVE: You haven't answered my question, darling!

TEMPLE: What question? You've been popping questions at me all the afternoon! Oh – Oh, about Myers. Well, you see, Myers called himself Cartwright for a short while whilst he was working on a special case for the F.B.I. Ricky happened to be working at the hotel where he was staying. Myers is an odd bird, completely reliable but he simply won't take anyone into his confidence. Now, for instance, the night when they arrested Mrs Trevelyan, Myers was scared to death that I'd accept that Mrs Trevelyan was ALEX and abandon the case. But, in spite of this, instead

187

of coming along to the house and putting his cards on the table he …

STEVE: He told you that he'd seen Chester put the cyanide in the flask and he produced a note …

TEMPLE: Which was supposed to have been written by ALEX. Of course he knew darn well that Chester <u>had</u> put the cyanide in the flask – no-one else could have done it – but the note … was just a little ruse to keep me interested in the case. But I'd already tumbled to the fact that the girl in brown was working with him.

STEVE: But that night we went out to Claywood Hill …

TEMPLE: Chester followed us. Working under instructions from Lathom, he had already taken Leo there during the afternoon. As soon as Chester started to tail us, Davis – or Myers rather – tailed Chester …

STEVE: … And Sir Graham and Crane tailed Davis!

TEMPLE: Yes! And, by Timothy, it was a lucky thing for us they did.

STEVE: Yes. But what puzzles me is that phone call – that was supposed to be from Leo …

TEMPLE: That was intended to put me off the scent, Steve. To turn my attention away from Chester and the hotel.

STEVE: But, if they thought that call would keep you <u>away</u> from the hotel, how did they expect you to find the note they put in Leo's room? It was obviously planted there before we arrived – so how could they have known the phone call hadn't worked?

TEMPLE: Don't you see, Steve? I rang the hotel to book a room.

STEVE: Oh! … (*Slight pause*) Yes … I ought to have thought of that.

TEMPLE: (*Pulling STEVE's leg*) Yes, darling – you really ought to have thought of that! Steve, are you going to eat those scones?

STEVE: Paul, you've had three already!

TEMPLE: (*Eating*) Just another one, darling!

STEVE: You said that two scones ago – and don't talk with your mouth full …

TEMPLE: You know, I can't help feeling rather pleased with myself over this case, Steve. Did you see what the London Mercury said this morning?

STEVE: Yes, I did.

TEMPLE: It described me as Europe's foremost detective. Private-Eye Number One!

STEVE: Yes, well – what I'd like to know is, when is Private-Eye Number One going to do some work for a change?

TEMPLE: What do you mean – work?

STEVE: I mean – work! You're a writer: and you're supposed to finish your new novel by the end of the month!

TEMPLE: Yes, you're right! Dead right! And I've got some news for you! The moment I've finished this scone – and that one too, darling, if you don't want it – I'm going to go into the study, get out the old typewriter, and start bashing away at …

The telephone rings.

STEVE: It's all right. I'll take it.

STEVE lifts the receiver.

STEVE: (*On the phone*) Hello?

FORBES: (*On the other end of the line*) Steve? …

STEVE: Oh, hello, Sir Graham!

FORBES: Can I have a word with Temple?

STEVE: He's – He's not here at the moment. Is there anything I can do?

FORBES: No, I don't think so, Steve. Look, get him to ring me back, as soon as he comes in!

STEVE: Is it – er – a new case, Sir Graham?

FORBES: (*With enthusiasm*) It is indeed. Absolutely fascinating. Just Temple's cup of tea. Don't forget, Steve – get him to ring me the moment he comes in!

STEVE: I'll do that, Sir Graham. It'll be just after Christmas.

FORBES: Just after Christmas?

STEVE: Yes – he's gone away for several months.

FORBES: Gone away … Where?

STEVE: I don't know, Sir Graham – but I'm expecting to hear from him at any moment! Bye …

STEVE replaces the receiver.

TEMPLE: What is this? What's the big idea telling Sir Graham that I've gone away for six months?!

STEVE: (*Pointing; with authority*) To the study!

TEMPLE: Steve, I want to know what Sir Graham …

STEVE: TO THE STUDY!

TEMPLE: (*A sigh*) Oh – very well …

STEVE: (*Relenting*) And you can take the scones with you, darling.

TEMPLE: (*Laughing*) Thank <u>you</u>, Mrs Temple.

FADE IN closing music.

THE END

Press Pack

Press cuttings about Paul Temple and the Alex Affair

40 Talent-Spotting Years At The BBC by **Charles Hatton**
Martyn C. Webster, former regional drama and variety
producer, retires from the BBC after tonight's *Saturday
Night Theatre production*. He has given forty years' service,
and for six years before the second World War, he effected
many changes in Midland Broadcasting.

On my first visit to the BBC Midland studios in 1933,
they struck me as a small oasis of culture and bonhomie in
the midst of a tough materialist conurbation.

My purpose was to interview Martyn C. Webster, the
newly arrived variety producer, for a weekly periodical, and
it was typical of this slim, fresh complexioned young man
that before I had been in his office ten minutes he had
discovered I wrote material for concert parties and was
urging me to try my hand on book and lyrics for a radio
revue.

He had that rare gift of generating enthusiasm, and I can
say without fear of contradiction that no one has fostered
more young talent since the B.B.C. came into existence. In a
matter of weeks after his arrival, the Midland studios were
humming with activity as he produced one musical show
after another.

Soon he was encouraged to embark on straight plays as
well; as a result he brought to light the work of a nineteen
year old university student named Francis Durbridge, who
wrote several plays and musicals for Webster, before
embarking upon the hitherto untried venture of an original
radio serial which launched Paul Temple on his adventures,
which have lasted more than 30 years.

Among his other major discoveries in Birmingham were:

Marjorie Westbury, whom he heard mimicking a music hall star in the canteen. He gave her an audition and a number of leading parts as a result.

Edward J. Mason from Cadbury's advertising department.

Jack Hill, a rent collector for Birmingham Corporation, and a pianist-composer of great talent.

Wilfred Southworth, another composer, who was a cinema organist at Handsworth.

Dorothy Summers, later a national figure as Mrs Mopp of *I.T.M.A.*

John Bentley, the actor of *Crossroads* fame, who gave Webster his first audition while still a schoolboy.

R.D. Smith, then a university student, now a successful radio producer.

The list seems endless, and incidentally includes a fair proportion of the present cast of *The Archers*.

He formed the *Radio Follies* concert party which ran for several years, and his radio versions of West End musicals were soon in demand by the national network. These he presented in collaboration with the Malvern musical director, Reginald Burston, who was to conduct many Drury Lane shows in the post-war years.

For weeks at a time, Martyn Webster was in or around the Midland studios for twelve hours every day – no new experience for him, because when he first joined the B.B.C. in Glasgow in 1926 he was required to clock-in at 9.30 a.m. and remain on duty as relief announcer, wearing a dinner jacket until midnight, in addition to his production duties.

In those days he had an agreeable light baritone voice, and when the famous Co-Optimists visited the Midland studios for a broadcast, he deputised at short notice for

Melville Gideon, who suddenly became ill. But he was always a rather nervous performer, and it usually took some such emergency to bring him before the microphone.

During his stay in the Midlands, Webster organised a popular series of cabaret broadcasts from Welcome Hotel, Stratford-upon-Avon, a new departure for Midland broadcasts in those days. He exerted his considerable powers of persuasion to induce many famous performers to give their services in return for a luxury weekend in Warwickshire.

Like many another producer he made an occasional error in casting, but the majority of shows had an unmistakable *brio*, which was the result of assiduous application to detail. After a rehearsal, he would single out the weakest performer and take him or her back to the office where they would run over the lines until both were satisfied.

He was always ready to listen to an actor's or a writer's personal problems and to offer advice. On one occasion he had been hesitating between two actors for a part in a series, and eventually gave it to an actor who had told him a hard-luck story and even threatened suicide. Having secured his contract, the actor calmly walked down Broad Street and ordered another expensive suit for his already overflowing wardrobe.

After he entered the maelstrom of wartime broadcasting, where he produced dozens of programmes from various secret headquarters, Webster never returned to the Midlands. He became a full-time drama producer and gave up his musical shows working at Broadcasting House in London. Some time after the start of post-war television he produced two successful Francis Durbridge serials, launching him on a new career as a writer for television.

But Martyn Webster felt that television presented too many headaches for a middle-aged producer, and thought it was a medium more suited to the younger producer. So he eventually returned to sound radio, where his output was soon as prolific as ever.

He was recently at the controls for the production of Francis Durbridge's new serial *La Boutique*, specially written for the European Broadcasting Union, an appropriate swan song to this thirty-year-old partnership of writer and producer.

On The Other Hand, Martyn Webster's final *Saturday Night Theatre* production tonight, reaches the microphone only after a certain amount of frustration. Basil Douglas, who adapted it from a story by Gerald Kersh, took the script away with him on holiday to Austria, and wrote most of it when cut off by a heavy snowstorm. On the way home, the boot of his car was broken into and his luggage stolen – including the script.

He had resigned himself to starting the job all over again when one evening there was a knock at his door, and two foreign gentlemen introduced themselves as Interpol detectives. After some detailed questioning, they agreed that his luggage should be restored to him, script included, thus saving weary hours of extra work.

Most B.B.C. producers retire at 60, but Martyn Webster's services were so continually in demand that, year on year, he was persuaded to postpone it, until eventually he reached the extreme limit. So he leaves the B.B.C. as its oldest producer; when he joined in 1926 he was its youngest.

Such talents in the field of creative production should not be lost to the entertainment world, and it's good to know that he will probably be joining a well-known international concert agency.   **Birmingham Post, 26 October 1967**

194

An' It Don't Seem A Day Too Much
Martyn C. Webster writes about Francis Durbridge's new Paul Temple story …

More than thirty years ago, as a young man – a very young man – Francis Durbridge had already written several musical comedies for radio, and dozens of sketches and lyrics for topical revues – all of them written with his characteristic competence and zest. But although his name was well known and his work was already being broadcast in many countries, he was hankering after something else. And eventually I found out what it was.

As an avid reader of just about every play ever published, he had become something of a stage encyclopaedia, but there was another for whom he had a great admiration. One day he said to me "If only I could be half as good as Edgar Wallace." I was surprised as I thought Wallace rather dated. Durbridge would not agree; he considered him the best craftsman in his class. A million copies of his books were re-issued shortly afterwards!

"So that's what you have been hankering after; you want to write detective stories?" I asked. "I'm afraid I do," he replied. "Well, I have a hankering in the same direction: I've always wanted to produce a serial with an original radio detective. I'm tired of adaptations of Sherlock Holmes and so on. So why not have a shot at creating an original radio sleuth?"

He just smiled. But next morning he rang me. "I've been thinking it over and I'd like to have a shot. In fact I've already thought of a name – Paul Temple – how does it sound to you?" It sounded just right to me, and it must have sounded 'just right' to listeners too, for on the morning after the broadcast of our first episode we had over seven thousand letters asking for more.

And so Francis Durbridge realised his ambition, and became a writer of detective stories whose hero was to become known all over the world. And I have been lucky enough to be the producer of all the Paul Temple serials. But in recent years Durbridge was so busy on his television and film work, and it has been almost impossible to get a new Temple serial.

Last October I was due to retire and was sad at the thought that I would never produce another 'Temple'. But the week before I actually did retire, Durbridge came into my office carrying a parcel. "A little present for you," he said. I opened it and found the scripts of a new Temple serial.

"You're a little late," I said, "I will not be here to produce it." "Oh yes you will," he replied, "the Powers That Be have agreed that you can. After all, it will be the thirtieth anniversary." Thirty years! I could hardly believe it – but it was true.

Paul and Steve have had many adventures since 1938; and somehow they still manage to stay as young and enterprising as ever they were. So let's hope they will give the same excitement to their many old friends and to lots of new ones as well.

Radio Times, 22 February 1968

Thirty Years Radio Partnership

Thirty years ago – in 1938 – an elegant and ingenious character called Paul Temple was introduced to listeners and he immediately became a public hero. His creator was a young Yorkshire author, Francis Durbridge, and his first serial was given to Martyn C. Webster to produce. Their partnership has persisted and has become one of the greatest success stories of radio.

Paul Temple is not only the favourite detective of generations of listeners here but his fame has spread all over the world and his adventures have been translated into many languages.

On the eve of his retirement from the B.B.C. staff, Mr Webster received an appropriate surprise. "We'd been trying to get Durbridge to write another Temple story for ages," Mr Webster says (the last was in 1965) "and just before I was due to leave he handed me the new manuscript with a grin. I was delighted, and I think it's one of the best he's done."

Paul Temple and the Alex Affair begins on February 26th. Durbridge is adept at creating situations which finish excitingly. He creates characters you can believe in – not cardboard people – and he goes to great trouble to verify every single detail.

Durbridge's success goes on: *La Boutique* which started a new pattern of twice-weekly serials at the beginning of B.B.C.'s Radio 1 and 2 will be repeated shortly, and his stories have been equally successful on television – the latest being *Bat Out of Hell*.

The Cork Examiner

Paul Temple Opens His Last Radio Case

It all began with a sketch at a university revue. Its quality made an immediate impression on a member of the audience, just "an interested observer" named Martyn C. Webster of the B.B.C.

Afterwards he met the actor-author and asked if he would be interested in writing for radio. He was. And so started one of the most successful drama partnerships broadcasting has known.

The writer was Erdington born Francis Durbridge. This occasion marked the start of a career that was to earn him a

197

world-wide reputation as a writer of thrillers for radio and television.

He created radio's first ace detective, Paul Temple. This was after Mr Webster accepted the script of his first play *Promotion*.

Birmingham was Temple's first home. *Send For Paul Temple* was launched here in 1938 with Martyn C. Webster as producer. He has been in charge of all the twenty-one series that followed. The last was heard three years ago.

In recent years Francis Durbridge has devoted more of his time to television. He has achieved equal success with television-thrillers.

Now they are to put the seal on a thriving association. When Mr Webster was due to retire last October, he said that he was sorry it had not been possible to persuade Mr Durbridge to write one more detective series.

He was wrong. Temple's creator handed him the manuscript of *Paul Temple and the Alex Affair*. This eight-part thriller starts its twice-weekly run tonight on Radio 2. Martyn Webster stayed on to produce it.

Production of Paul Temple moved from Birmingham to London in 1941.

Peter Coke takes up again the Temple role, and Marjorie Westbury resumes duty as the unflappable Steve, his wife.

Since 1938 there have only been two "Steves" – Bernadette Hodgson and Miss Westbury.* Mr Coke is the seventh Paul Temple.

Birmingham Evening Mail, 26 February 1968

* Although only Misses Hodgson and Westbury played Steve in the radio serials, Thea Holme and Lucille Lisle each played Steve in one-hour radio abridgements.

Paul Temple by **Gillian Reynolds** (contains spoilers)

He writes successful novels but is better known for his criminal connections. His favourite drink is a dry, a very dry martini. He is intelligent, assured, sophisticated, compassionate, and he always has been blissfully married to an intelligent and attractive lady called Steve. If you are over twenty-five you will no doubt by this time have recognised Paul Temple, thirty this year, and the B.B.C.'s longest established serving hero.

Listening to *Coronation Scot* last week opening Francis Durbridge's latest Temple serial, *Paul Temple and the Alex Affair*, had an extraordinary effect on me. When I was ten or so that music heralded a magic transformation into a clear sophisticated world, where Paul and Steve sipped well-chilled cocktails served by their servant, Charlie, where Sir Graham Forbes of Scotland Yard always sent for Paul Temple when the going got tricky, where Paul's incisive mind picked up every one of the carefully strewn clues the precisely right number of steps ahead of the audience. Paul was then being played by Kim Peacock, Marjorie Westbury then as now was Steve, but the most amazing thing about the new serial is that only the plot has changed. The Temples still live in a timeless world, only Paul's references to Steve's pretty hats have a slightly dated ring. They haven't aged a day themselves.

Last week's adventure began with the discovery of a body on a train, a cryptic scrawl "Alex" on the compartment window, and the discovery of a visiting card bearing the name "Mrs Trevelyan." More bodies, more "Alex" inscriptions, and more pieces of paper with "Mrs Trevelyan" written on them; and Paul, at first reluctantly, becomes increasingly involved. In the second episode, Paul is lured by Mrs Trevelyan herself to her house where by seconds (and characteristic astuteness) he narrowly escapes being blown up by a bomb in a suitcase. He leaves to keep an urgent nocturnal rendezvous with Sir Graham and a Dutch crook called Muller but when they find Muller he is lying with his throat cut in a pool blood. Steve, having made her own way home after the bomb incident, has been followed and by a girl – "Quite smart – brown shoes – brown suit – brown handbag – perky little hat … quite smart, darling."

Francis Durbridge is, of course, an established master of the thriller. His last television serial, *Bat Out of Hell*, has just been rerun and was one of a few BBC programmes to appear in the TAM ratings. All over Europe, on radio, television, and in Germany on the stage, his work commands an enormous following. Everywhere his work has been seen he has managed to do the impossible by being at once a tremendous public and critical success. Martyn C. Webster, an elegant, slightly elfin figure who smokes forty untipped cigarettes a day, has been the producer of Paul Temple from the first. He discovered Francis Durbridge at the age of twenty in a revue at Birmingham University. He was not, says Mr Webster, an engaging performer. "In fact his performance was so bad that he stood out; then I saw he was the writer of most of the sketches …" And his material in the revue was impressive. Asked for a further sample he turned up with a play, *Promotion*, which was broadcast and repeated twelve times.

But, said Mr Webster, he hankered for something else, to create an original radio detective. That was the beginning of Paul Temple. It was an immediate success, and Paul Temple was asked to go to television. Durbridge refused, believing that pace and impression of the Temple style was impossible to translate.

That, perhaps, is one of the reasons Paul Temple is still with us on radio today. We have never seen him, so his seven separate incarnations in actors as diverse as Carl

Bernard, Barry Morse, and Howard Marion Crawford don't divert us.

Paul (now Peter Coke) retains his integrity as a character. Mr Durbridge's neat hand with a plot is a continuing reason for appreciation.

In so firmly establishing Paul and Steve Temple over all these years in their own world and in making that world a timeless one, Mr Durbridge has cannily protected his investment. In the continuity of Martyn C. Webster's production we have been able to enjoy it all the more. In a fitting tribute to a long-standing and friendly creative partnership, in fact, Mr Durbridge arranged for Mr Webster to stay on after his retirement last October to produce this latest Paul Temple.

The Guardian

Printed in Great Britain
by Amazon

40801894R00128